Arctic Memories

The Sod Hut

Arctic Memories
THE SOD HUT

WRITERS REPUBLIC L.L.C.
515 Summit Ave. Unit R1
Union City, NJ 07087, USA

Website: *www.writersrepublic.com*
Hotline: *1-877-656-6838*
Email: *info@writersrepublic.com*

Ordering Information:
Quantity sales. Special discounts are available on quantity purchases by corporations, associations, and others. For details, contact the publisher at the address above.

Library of Congress Control Number:		2020940995
ISBN-13:	978-1-64620-574-5	[Paperback Edition]
	978-1-64620-460-1	[Digital Edition]

Rev. date: 08/06/0000

Arctic MEMORIES

THE SOD HUT

BY

WENDELL AMISIMAK STALKER

CONTENTS

ESKIMO DOG TEAM HUNTING

CIRCA EARLY 1900S

By Wendell Amisimak Stalker

5-6-2018

This is a work of fiction. Names, characters, places and incidents are either the product of the author's imagination or are used fictitiously, and any resemblance to actual persons, living or dead, business establishments, events or locales is entirely coincidental.

My name is Spring Flood. I had been named after one of the worse years the people have ever lived through. We had moved inland from our yearly spring and summer hunt along the coast, and winter had come early. Then after a long cold winter with a lot of wind and blowing snow, the people had been caught out in the open as we moved to the ocean. My mother got sick and I was born. She had lived for three days after I was born, then quietly passed on.

My father, Sharp Tip, had taken me to his younger sister and the only thing he told her was my name. Swan Swims Around was the one who raised me and I called her Mom. Her husband was a good hunter and was happy to have a son. His name is Walking In Fast. I called him Poppa.

The years flew by in a blur. I learned a lot about how to hunt and Poppa taught me how to make my own tools. I needed them to build sleds, boats, and things for the home. He was very patient with me and helped me make harnesses for seven dogs. He showed me how to bind the sled. We put one together using wooden pegs and rawhide. He jumped with joy when I went on my first dog team ride with seven dogs I had raised up. I had done odd jobs and asked for pups as payment. He had helped me train the young dogs and I knew my world was about to get bigger.

We are Inupiaq and we lived above the Arctic Circle. There were around 80 people in our village and most of us went hunting and fishing in spring down the coast. We then moved back inland to our village set in some trees, about 50 miles into the river. Though over land, the ocean was about 15 miles away to the west. The mountains were high, and using the river was the easiest way to go back and forth every year.

I was 14 when I first helped move to the coast with my dog team. Poppa and I were taking a load of trout and long thin poles for making fish traps. My sled had seven gunny sacks of rainbow trout. Poppa's sled had 20 long dried poles piled on his sled. The poles were not heavy but stuck out the back six feet and he had to run alongside the sled.

I followed behind Poppa and he soon was way ahead. He had told me not to let my young dogs get tired and watch them carefully. He went up the side of the mountain and stopped. I just kept the young dogs going slow but steady. I could see Poppa up ahead waiting for me.

When I pulled up to him he smiled and pointed west. I looked and saw the vast Arctic Ocean. The ice went on for miles and miles with black dots here and there. Poppa told me the black dots were seals laying up on the ice.

He let me check all my dogs' feet. He gave me little booties and he showed me how to tie them on each foot. He put booties on all my dogs.

After that he pulled out his thermos and we had a cup of hot tea. While we were sitting on my sled drinking tea, we noticed a herd of muskoxen running down below us and towards the ocean. They came running out from a hidden valley between the mountains. Soon they stopped running and quickly formed a circle on a little rise. The smaller muskoxen were kept in the middle and the rest of the herd made a protective circle around them.

Then we saw five big wolves come out from the valley and go to the herd of muskoxen. The muskoxen didn't run anymore, they had picked their spot and held their ground. The wolves circled them, but when they got too close, one of the big male muskoxen would try to hook them, then quickly move back and filled the gap. All the muskoxen faced out and soon the wolves sat down about 50 yards away and studied the herd.

Poppa quickly put the thermos away and told me to follow him. We both held our lead dogs and walked down the side of the mountain. We went around a big rock and stopped. Poppa told me to wait there with the dogs while he walked as close as he could to the wolves and try to get a shot. He told me to check on him only after he shot because he didn't want to scare the wolves.

I sat there with the dogs and waited. I sure wanted to go look but Poppa told me to stay with the two sleds and our dogs. The dogs were all very quiet. I think they could smell the wolves.

I was south of the big rock that hid me and the dog teams from the herd of muskoxen. I could smell a musky odor and that alone would have made the dogs excited, relating the smell with meat. There was a gentle breeze coming from the north.

I looked west and saw many black dots. The ice was covered in snow as were the mountains. There were spruce trees that covered some of the lower hills, but mostly it was all barren tundra. We were at the western end of the Brooks Range mountains and were about a hundred miles above the Arctic Circle. We were traveling west going through a mountain pass in as straight a line as possible from the village to the ocean.

As I was looking at the ocean, I saw an Arctic Fox run zigzagging up the mountain to the south. I watched as it went back and forth on a ledge with brown grass on it. Then it stopped and started digging. Soon it pulled something that was buried out and set that down. It then started going back and forth again until it stopped and again dug in the ground. Soon it pulled something out and carried it to the first thing it dug up. Fixing both in his mouth, he picked them up and trotted back into the mountains.

It was not too long after that I heard Poppa's rifle. I quickly walked around the big rock and saw Poppa taking aim at a big gray wolf running in front of three others. He shot and the big gray went down. Then in another second I heard another shot and one brown wolf went down. The other two went around a big bunch of willows and disappeared.

I went back to the dog teams and waited. Soon Walking In Fast came running around the big rock. He put his rifle in his gun pouch that was tied alongside his sled.

"Let's go over now," he said, as he reached down and picked up his brake hook. He led the way to where he had shot from and stopped on the side of the mountain. I pulled up alongside of him and set my hook in the hard frozen snow.

"Wait here. I will walk down this way and get the three wolves, OK?" Poppa said, as he pulled out his pistol and a length of rawhide rope.

I sat with the dogs as he walked to the farthest one. He tied the line around the neck and dragged it to the next one. That next one was the big gray. He attached the line and dragged both to a gray wolf that was smaller than the big gray. He dragged all three down to the bottom of the valley. He quit pulling the three wolves when he was under me, about 90 feet down. He unraveled the rawhide rope as he climbed up to me.

I met him half way and we slowly pulled the three wolf carcasses up. Working together, we got all three up to the ledge we were on. When we pulled them up, all the dogs got scared. They seemed to get smaller in front of my eyes.

"It's OK," said Poppa, in a soothing voice.

We tied all three on top of the wood. Poppa then pulled out the thermos and some dried caribou. We had a bite and enjoyed a cup of hot tea.

"The first shot they were all looking at the muskoxen. I got the one that was farthest and watched the big one lead the others. I then shot him, then the dark brown one. I could see it better with the snow in the background. The other two ran into the willows. They were both gray." He told me between bites of dried caribou and drinks of tea.

The muskoxen are still there," I said, chewing.

"They have chosen that rise and won't move until all the danger is gone. The muskoxen have been protecting their young like that for who knows how long. They will probably be doing that when your grandchildren come this way," said Poppa, chewing on a piece of tasty caribou.

"I saw a fox dig two animals across there. On the other mountain over on that grassy part there," I said, as I pointed where I had seen the fox.

"It probably have a lot more up there. He just got enough for himself. That should keep the fox fed for two or three days. They know how to live through long winters. We do the same. We are going to bring these trout to our underground cellar. When we hunt in the spring and summer there will be food from the river to go with all the foods from the sea," said Poppa.

We finished our tea break and I followed Poppa going down the side of the mountain at an angle. We slowly went down, both of us, with our foot on the foot break and our weight on the left runner. The dogs stayed in a straight line and we talked to them and when the trail finally leveled out we let the dogs run.

I could feel the wind on my face and we stayed on the trail. Sometimes it went like a big S, but it was smooth going on the trail. The dogs slowed in their own time and just settled into a trot. The older dogs of Poppa could keep it at that pace all day long, but I slowed my young dogs down and again saw Poppa pull ahead.

Soon Poppa went down the last hill and I was alone. I could hear the sled runners gentle whistle and see the breath coming from each dog. The dogs wanted to go faster but I kept them going at a steady trot. My leader would look back at me once in a while like he expected me to give the order to speedup.

After going down the last hill, the trail turned north. I saw smoke up ahead. I slowly pulled up to the camp and Poppa came and showed me where he wanted the fish. I let the dogs stop when the sled was next to the cellar door. The cellar was underground and stayed frozen all year long.

Poppa opened the cellar door and climbed down the ladder. He stopped about ten feet down. The underground cellar was dug into the permafrost and the room was ten by twelve, with the ladder in the middle.

I carried a full gunnysack of trout to the ladder and tied the line on. Then I slowly fed the line and lowered the sack of fish to Poppa's waiting arms. He balanced the gunnysack on one knee and the ladder and untied the rope. He moved the bag over to one side while I pulled the rope up and got it ready for the next sack of frozen trout. The sled was right there so I just tied the rope on the next bag and pulled the loose line over my shoulder. I used a slip knot so Poppa just had to yank on the end of the rope and it would be free from the gunnysack.

We unloaded the sled and tied all the dogs on two long chains. I then cut some salmon for each of them. I used an ax to cut the salmon in pieces. The salmon was half dried. And I also gave each dog some water. There were still several bags of salmon we put in the cellar the year before. Poppa had me give each dog a six inch strip of seal blubber. After I fed all the dogs, I went into the tent and took my warm clothes off.

Poppa was cooking caribou rice and gravy and it really smelled good. He had the two-burner primer stove on and the ten by twelve canvas tent was already warm. There was a wood stove, but Poppa didn't light that. We used the wood stove mostly in the morning, after a cold night.

There was a flock of white snowbirds that lived around the camp. As I sat there watching Poppa cook the meat and gravy, a couple landed on the tent. Poppa pointed up at them and he smiled.

I could see the birds' shadow on the white canvas tent. They danced around before suddenly taking flight. Their shadows hit the bottom of the tent and they were gone.

"I like to hear the birds chirping," said Poppa as he stirred the rice.

"Yes, they are good to listen to," I said as I went to the grub box and pulled out our plates and spoons. I pulled the biscuits out Mom had baked for us. With the butter and jam they would be good with what Poppa was cooking.

"Their little feet sure could cling to the tent," said Poppa as he turned the primer stove off.

We filled our plates with steaming hot rice and gravy. I added a teaspoon of seal oil in mine and sprinkled a little salt and pepper on, and filled my cup with tundra tea. I put butter and jam on my biscuit and enjoyed the first meal of the year on the coast.

"After we rest we will go out on the ice and hunt seals. There are a lot of seals on the ice out there and we should be able to fill our sleds before going home," said Poppa while we ate until we were full to the neck.

It was still really bright out. In the spring and early summer the sun stays up 24 hours a day. The white canvas tent we were in reflected the sunlight and I put my arm over my eyes. I thought about the fox I had seen on the other mountain while waiting for Poppa to shoot the wolves. That fox was the smart one, hiding food for a long, cold winter.

Poppa sat on his sleeping bag and took his mukluks off. He set them aside, after making sure they were dry. He looked at me laying there and smiled.

"Let me tell you about the first time I helped my father, Plenty Skins. It was much the same as this, but back then we didn't have canvas tents, we used caribou skins and the frame was round. My younger brother, Marrow, and younger sister, Blooming Salmonberry, were with us, along with Plenty Skin's wife, Sews with Grass.

We were alone when we put the caribou skin on the driftwood frame. There were nine dogs tied in the back and Plenty Skins was repairing his kayak frame. The dogs started barking and I followed Plenty Skins out. He had his rifle, but it was not needed. The dogs were barking at another dog team that was coming from the north.

"They will be hungry," said Plenty Skins. "Go get caribou meat from the cellar, and the seal poke. Marrow, go help your brother, Sharp Tip. Come, Blooming Salmonberry, let's go heat more water for tea."

By the time we had the caribou meat and seal poke out of the underground cellar, the dog team stopped. The sled was piled high. Just as high as the men who ran alongside of it. I saw nine dogs pulling and only when they stopped did I notice the men had rawhide ropes tied to the sled and used those to help the dogs move the sled.

Plenty Skins came out of our caribou skin tent and walked up to them. He shook hands and welcomed them to our summer hunting camp.

Marrow and I were dragging the seal poke over to the tent. It was full of seal oil and different kinds of meat and greens from the tundra. One of the men walked over to us and said, "Hi, let me get that." He picked it up and slung it across his right shoulder and asked, "Where you want it?"

I looked at my brother, Marrow, and was in awe at his strength. I mumbled something and pointed to the tent, holding the heavy seal poke like it was not any problem at all. Marrow and I followed him in. He set it on the floor and turned to Blooming Salmonberry and smiled and went back out without saying a word. My mom, Sews With Grass, sat on the floor watching the kettle of water and looked at me as if to ask who he was. I shrugged my shoulders and went back out with Marrow at my side.

Plenty Skins was helping the other man put out a line so he could tie his dogs. He held a four-foot post while the other man dug a hole. After he went down a couple feet, they put one end in and put the gravel back in to hold it in place.

They had another post about 40 feet away and had a long chain laid out. The man tied the chain on the post they had just put in. He then started tying each dog to a four-foot length of chain that was attached to the main line.

The other man had started untying the load on the sled. When I saw him moving back and forth around the sled untying the line, I went on one side and helped him. He smiled but didn't say anything.

When we got done untying the line he went to the front of the sled and pulled out a gunnysack. He quickly untied the line and pulled out some half-dried salmon. The fish was then cut up with an ax and he gave a piece to each of the barking dogs. He also pulled out nine feeding bowls and filled each with water from our water barrel used for dogs.

Finally they got them fed and watered with grass under each dog so they wouldn't have to sleep on the snow. 'Then we all went into our tent. The two men were both too tall to stand straight, they both bent their heads down and started taking their warm parkas off. They took their warm parkas off and sat on the floor.

The older man had tattoos on his face and an ivory labret under the right side of his mouth. He had a big nose and I was surprised to see hair on his chin.

The other man was younger without tattoos or a labret. At first I couldn't get what was different about them sitting there until I looked at Poppa. I then noticed Poppa's heels were touching the floor where he sat and I looked at the two men and saw both their heels were not touching the floor. I then realized their calf muscles were so big that they held their heels off the floor. Those guys were travelers and had built up their leg muscles just walking everywhere.

"My name is Over The Horizon and this young man is my nephew, Wind Blowing Clouds. We are traders and are on our way south to trade with the people at the trading village of Port Walrus. We were there four years ago and promised to bring our trade goods before the ice is gone. We plan on going back up north with a skin boat," said the older man as he accepted a bowl full of caribou soup my mother had cooked.

Wind Blowing Clouds smiled and said, "Thank you, that smells really good."

Sews With Grass made sure everyone was served, then sat by Plenty Skins. Everybody got quiet while we ate until Over The Horizon set his plate aside and gave a loud burp. Plenty Skins smiled and asked, "Is there anything else you two would like to eat?"

"We came this way four years ago and I caught a seal out there. It was enough for one meal because we fed our eleven dogs and it was a small seal. I stretched the skin and left it on your drying rack," said Over The Horizon with a smile on his face.

"I wondered where that skin came from," said Sews With Grass.

"Look, she made a poke out of it because there was no hole on the whole seal skin," said Plenty Skins, as he pointed at the seal poke that Wind Blowing Clouds had carried in.

"I had Wind Blowing Clouds make a big circle all around me while I waited at a breathing hole with a club. I stood there until that seal poked his head out of the water. Then I just clubbed it and skinned it starting at the mouth. I then filled it with air and tied it shut. Then I tied it up there on that drying rack," said the trader.

"What do I owe you?" asked Plenty Skins.

"No. It is I who need to pay for hunting on your land," said Over The Horizon.

"Now my grandfather, Ptarmigan Strut, would not let anyone pay to hunt this land," said Plenty Skins.

"Wait, did you say your grandfather's name is Ptarmigan Strut?" asked Over The Horizon with his eyes really big and looking straight into Plenty Skins' eyes.

"Yes, he's my grandfather on my father's side," said Poppa.

"Then we are relatives because Ptarmigan Strut is my grandfather on my mother's side of the family," said Over The Horizon, as he stood up to give Poppa Plenty Skins a brotherly hug.

"We are related," said Wind Blowing Clouds, as he gave me a hug.

Everyone got excited and my sister, Blooming Salmonberry, finally started talking and couldn't stop asking our new-found relatives about their life trading up and down the coast.

Marrow and I smiled and made sure Wind Blowing Clouds and Over The Horizon had everything they needed to get comfortable.

Soon we all moved outside and we helped them put their tent up. It was a big tent that could swallow four tents the size of ours and still have room to walk around inside between the four.

"We will trade this tent for a smaller one before we go back up North," said Over The Horizon.

When we went inside I could see a lot of drawings and paintings covering the whole tent. The sunlight made all the colors of the rainbow shine. There were people in winter and in summer, there was every animal from the North, there were birds and ducks and fish, along with all the other aquatic animals.

On one side there was a family waving goodbye to some people leaving in four skin boats. There were about 20 people leaving and all were waving back at the people on shore.

"That was the time when Ptarmigan Strut and his family left our village. I was a young boy then and I remember Ptarmigan Strut as he sat at the back of the first skin boat, steering with a bigger paddle," said Over The Horizon, pointing at the skin boats painted on the wall of the skin tent.

"This tent was a place where painters and carvers met. All the history of grandpa Ptarmigan Strut are shown. I had to pay a dear price for it and those skins and trade goods will be the last payment," said Over The Horizon.

"I'm very glad I have a chance to see all this," said Plenty Skins.

"I don't have to trade it for a smaller one anymore. I will just leave it to you, my cousin, and whenever I come this way it will be here for me to use," said Over The Horizon, as he gave us all a hug.

"Family is good," said Plenty Skins, as we walked on the inside of the tent, looking at all the stories.

The two men rested their dogs for a couple days and left in the middle of the night, when the snow was firm because of the night chill. We saw them again that summer as they stopped by in a skin boat. The same dogs that pulled the sled south in early spring now pulled the skin boat north. The two left many gifts and promised they would be back the next spring, but not to trade, to visit and get to know the rest of the family.

I was surprised when Over The Horizon gave me the .243 Winchester rifle with four boxes of shells. They gave a bolt of cloth with flower patterns to my Momma, Sews With Grass. Wind Blowing Clouds gave Blooming Salmonberry a hand held mirror and a hair brush. He gave a .22 Ruger to Marrow with four boxes of shells. Over The Horizon gave Poppa a set of steel traps for wolves and wolverine and smaller traps for muskrat. Plenty Skins was so happy with the steel traps and all the gifts our relatives gave to us. He pulled out his drum and Over The Horizon pulled his out and we had a dance right there on the beach.

Plenty Skins and Over The Horizon started by singing one of grandpa Ptarmigan Strut's favorite songs. Wind Blowing Clouds danced and we saw the story of Ptarmigan Strut's first grizzly bear hunt.

We danced to the beat of the Ancient Ones. The songs and motions of dancers brought to life the old memories. We danced the old songs that were handed down from before the People had metal. We let the mountains and Arctic Ocean hear the words that were first sang five hundred years ago.

The knowledge and wisdom of the old ones was passed along through song and dance. We let the world know that we are alive and when we go, our young people will dance our songs of life.

When we went to our tent we put our gifts away and each went to bed with smiles and full bellies. I put my .243 Winchester rifle with Poppa's and put one box of shells in the grub box and the other three boxes in my duffel bag, after I put them in an empty bag. I lay on my bed and couldn't help but smile and feel all bubbly inside.

When I woke up, it was early in the morning. I lay inside my sleeping bag and listened. It was very quiet and there was no wind. The sun shone from the northeast and I could hear snowbirds and seagulls. I slowly got up trying not to wake anyone. The only one who moved was Poppa. He rolled, but didn't wake up.

I picked up my mukluks on the way out of the caribou skin tent and put them on after I went outside. As I was tying the mukluks, I noticed movement from the corner of my eye. I looked out towards the Arctic Ocean and saw many Eider ducks flying low over the water, all headed north. They were in lines, with one family making one line. And there were hundreds of flocks in wave after wave. The only time they flew higher was over the bigger icebergs, otherwise they flew low over the calm water.

It was a beautiful and quiet morning. If it wasn't for the birds chirping and seagulls piercing cries, it would have been quiet. I looked up and down the coast and saw geese coming from the south. As I was looking at geese flying high, I heard something take a deep breath of air. I quickly went to the grub box and pulled out the box of .243 shells and picked my new rifle up. I walked out onto the ice and started looking for whatever had come up from the bottom of the ocean and take a deep breath as soon as it surfaced.

I put shells in the rifle and put it on safety. I then walked slowly to a low ridge where there was open water just on the other side. I slowly looked over the ridge and saw a huge walrus struggling to climb up on the ice. I put my rifle to my shoulder, but I didn't shoot. I watched the big brown and red walrus as it bounced the big belly onto the ice.

The huge walrus used three-foot long tusks to help pull the heavy stomach and tail out of the water. With a big splash of the tail and with front flippers and tusks pulling, the huge animal moved out of the water and onto the ice, the rolls of blubber going up and down while the beast moved away from the water. Water splashed off the big body as it slid to a stop about 15 feet away from the hole in the ice.

I put the front sight on the ear of the big walrus. I was about 20 yards away with my rifle resting on the ice ridge, laying on my stomach. I slowly put pressure on the trigger. When the rifle went off I knew I hit the ear because the huge walrus jumped straight up in the air about a feet then came crashing down. The 2,000 plus pounds broke some of the ice. The walrus lay where it landed. When the ice stopped moving, I could see water all around the walrus. It had broken apiece of ice about the size of a bedroom and was laying dead on a floating piece of ice.

I took the empty shell out of the barrel and made sure there was nothing inside the rifle barrel. I looked towards the tent and saw everyone hurrying to get to me. I waved to let them know everything was fine.

When Sews With Grass saw me wave she went back into the tent with Blooming Salmonberry. Poppa, Over The Horizon, and Wind

Blowing Clouds all had rifles in their hands as they came at a fast walk. Marrow came behind them as they climbed the ridge I was on.

We all looked down at the walrus and we started climbing down to it. When I got down lower I could see the broken ice it was on had moved out about a foot. There was open water on the other side of the floating ice.

Wind Blowing Clouds turned around and climbed back up the ridge and went back to camp to get his seal hook and another length of rawhide rope. He brought back Marrow's .22 rifle and told Marrow to watch the open water.

Marrow walked about 20 yards to the right and sat down and loaded his new .22 Ruger. He then got comfortable and sat watching the open water.

We jumped onto the ice and walked up to the huge walrus. We saw the tusks were about three feet long and it was about14 feet long from the head to the tail flippers. It was a fat, round walrus.

Over The Horizon took one end of the rawhide rope and, holding about four yards, he walked around the tail flippers. He pulled the rope under the walrus while Wind Blowing Clouds held the other end of the rope. They pulled together and moved the rope about 1/3 of the way and did it a couple more times, going from the back of the walrus and sliding the rope between the carcass and the ice. Then they moved to the front and pulled the rawhide rope under the walrus until they passed the shoulders.

All four of us pulled the huge carcass onto it's back. We then started cutting. I worked with Wind Blowing Clouds by sharpening his knives. He used two knives; I sharpened one while he cut with the other. When that got dull, he would exchange with the one I just sharpened. Both knives were good steel knives, but they would get dull from the tough walrus hide and blubber.

Poppa and Over The Horizon worked on the other end of the walrus, one cutting while the other sharpened.

I sharpened and sharpened all morning. We got done in about three hours. By then all the meat was tied within it's own blubber and skin. Wind Blowing Clouds cut all the way to the bone and cut roughly about 2-1/2 foot squares before separating the block from the carcass.

After we cut all the meat and blubber off with the skin, we cut one inch holes about three inches apart all around the edges of the skin, then put a rawhide rope through the holes and zigzagged across until we had a bundle of meat and fat all wrapped in the skin.

Over The Horizon put the stomach aside after he emptied the clams on the ice. He put all the clams with shells back into the huge stomach. The other clams that didn't have a shell, he put in the dogs' cooking pot. He put other parts of the walrus intestines in and added water and cooked a big pot of dog food.

We put most of the walrus bundles of meat, blubber-wrapped in the skin, down into our underground cellar. We cooked some for lunch and after the dog food cooled off we fed the dogs.

Wind Blowing Clouds helped Sews With Grass by sharpening her ulu. She cut the skin, blubber, and meat into pieces. She then put everything in a big pot and cooked it over an open fire. The fire was protected on three sides and was thirty yards away from the tent.

That day the last of the ice floated far out to sea. There were a few pieces of ice on the beach, but all the floating ice had been blown out by the east wind.

Over The Horizon and Wind Blowing Clouds hitched up the dogs to the skin boat and after giving us all a hug, they went back up north.

Wing Blowing Clouds walked with the dogs, holding a six-foot walking stick while Over The Horizon used a paddle in the back and kept the skin boat away from the beach.

I gave them one bundle of walrus and Marrow gave them 10 snow geese he had shot down by the mud flats. Over The Horizon had told us his favorite cooking oil was the fat of the snow goose. When I helped Marrow carry them to their skin boat, Over The Horizon was so happy he even asked Marrow if he wanted to follow them.

We tried to give them more, but they both said it would be too heavy and they had a long ways to go before reaching their home. If the weather held up, they should be home in two weeks traveling on the shoreline.

We stayed there until late fall, then Poppa, Momma, and Blooming Salmonberry started south with relatives who had a big boat and were from the same village we were from. After they left, Marrow and I worked on the sled and hoped for snow. Plenty Skins had told us what to bring on the sled. We were to bring the seal poke full of all kinds of meats from the ocean. There was Beluga muktuk, walrus meat, seal meat, Eider ducks, and two buckets of clams. After the poke was full of meat we poured seal oil until it was air free, then we tied a wooden plug on the mouth with rawhide, binding it tightly so no air would be able to go in.

We also brought six bundles of walrus meat and three bags of ducks. Each bag had 10 to 15 ducks. We brought a huge bundle of half-dried Arctic Char and our grub box. We put all that in our sled, all wrapped in a tarp, then tied down.

The snow didn't come for a week, but when it came we hitched up the nine dogs and picked up any trash we had left that summer and threw it into the open fire. We checked, then double checked the lock on the underground cellar. It was not a padlock, just a latch to keep the animals from going into the cellar and stealing our food.

We planned to come back with the dog team a few times this coming winter. Marrow and I loaded the sled that first morning it snowed. We just kept the small tent up and it was not until that night when the snow quit falling, we hitched the dogs back up and I walked all around the camp before we pulled the hand brake up and started the dogs over the snow. We moved about 50 yards before the snow got too deep, so I put a pair of snowshoes on and walked in front, breaking trail for the dogs. I stayed in front, breaking trail, for about an hour before we made it up high enough for the snow to harden. By then we had climbed 1/3 of the way up the pass; the snow froze at night and the sled full of meat didn't sink anymore.

Marrow sat on top of the load and I stood in the back of the sled. I rested after struggling to break trail. The sun was down behind the mountains, but there was a full moon out. The sled runners made a gentle crackling sound. We used Poppa's older dogs, while he took the younger ones in the boat. After the hard start over deep snow, the dogs would soon be enjoying the travel as much as Marrow and I. Their feet gently touched the snow as they pulled the 14-foot sled.

The trail was easy to follow because it was the only level place. As soon as we would leave the trail, it got very bumpy.

We stopped when we got to the top of the trail and looked down. We could see the village about 12 miles away. Marrow and I made it the rest of the way to the village without any trouble, and that was how it was when I first helped my family move to the coast with dog team," said Walking In Fast, as he finished the story of his first year driving dogs.

"I remember Full Sails, the son of Wind Blowing Clouds," I said as I drank the last of my tea. Even it was cold by then.

"He said he would come by this summer," said Walking In Fast.

He checked the wood stove, and fixed it all up so we'd just have to strike a match to it and it will start right up. When the stove was ready for morning, we went outside and used our outhouse. We then went to bed in our down sleeping bags. I had a polar bear hide under my sleeping bag and slept like it was summer.

I woke up a few hours later and quickly lit the wood stove and set the kettle on to heat up. I then jumped back in bed and smiled at Poppa when he woke up to a warm tent.

I got back up and waited for the water to heat up. I made hot coffee when the water boiled and set it aside. I put ¼ cup of cold water in after it had a chance to brew a little. I filled Poppa's cup and brought it to him. He stirred the batter for sourdough pancakes and had a slab of bacon ready to be sliced and cooked.

He turned the primer stove on and cooked the pancakes and bacon. All the cooking made the little tent really warm and I was wearing a t-shirt and jeans. We both were barefoot.

Soon the smell of cooking sourdough pancakes and sizzling bacon filled the tent. Poppa cooked a huge stack of pancakes and fried four eggs in the bacon grease. After he was done cooking, he turned the primer stove off and refilled our coffee cups before putting the coffee pot on the wood stove.

When both our plates were full of sourdough hotcakes, with two fried eggs on top and a half dozen slices of bacon, we both started eating. Drinking everything down with good coffee.

"I will show you the old way of hunting seals today," said Poppa while we were eating.

He put a fork full of hotcake in his mouth, chewed for a while, then drank some of his coffee.

"In the old days they didn't have guns. They still got many seals, whales, and walrus. When we go on the ice, I want you to sit and watch as I get a seal without a rifle," Poppa said as we ate a hardy breakfast.

When we were done eating, I quickly washed the few dishes and used a towel to dry them. I put them back in the grub box.

While I was doing that, Poppa made sandwiches and filled the thermos with fresh coffee. He put the thermos into the caribou pouch made to keep the coffee hot all day long. He sharpened the two seal harpoons and put the wooden cover over both tips.

After he made sure everything was sharp, he tied polar bear skins that he had cut to fit onto his left leg up to the hip, and another piece he tied to his left arm. He picked up one harpoon and walked in front. He was dressed in furs with the white polar bear skin tied to his left side.

`I put the other harpoon in the sled with Poppa's .243. I carried my .22-250 on my right shoulder with a white cover made from canvas over the rifle.

The sled we used was the smallest we had, and the harpoon stuck out on both ends. Poppa's .243 fit at an angle. We put our thermos, sandwiches, and extra shells in a bag and had that tied under the rifle.

Poppa carried the shorter harpoon and told me to find some place to sit and watch. I walked over to a high ridge and left the sled at the bottom as I climbed up with the binoculars and my .22-250. When I got on top I sat down, facing the Arctic Ocean.

There was ice as far as you could see. From the top of the ridge I had a clear view of the big seal Poppa had pointed out. From up there I watched as Poppa tested the wind so he could approach the seal from downwind. I put my pointer finger in my mouth and lifted it up in the air and felt the side facing the ocean get a chill. I then knew the wind was blowing from the seal to Poppa.

I watched as Poppa slowly made his way to the seal. When he had no more ridges to hide behind he held the spear in front of him an lay down on his left side. The polar bear hide he had tied on his left leg kept the cold away from his body and made it possible to move noiselessly across the ice and snow.

His clothes were dark against the white of the snow and ice. He did not try to hide that from the seal. He mimicked the movements of the seal as it slept in snatches on the ice, soaking in the rays of the sun. Poppa showed his full length to the seal and moved a little at a time. The white cloth he tied around the handle of the harpoon blended in with the surrounding ice.

Poppa moved his legs towards the seal then followed by lifting and sliding his upper body. He repeated the process, sliding closer to the big seal. He lifted his right mitten up in the air like the seal would when looking for danger, then put it down and move a few inches closer to the sleeping seal.

As I sat on the ridge I was glad Poppa made me put my caribou hoof snow goggles on. With my goggles on I could see and have my eyes protected from the bright sunlight reflecting off the snow and ice. The sun was northeast of us and came down on my right cheek as I watched Poppa inching his way to the seal.

Poppa and the seal were in plain sight about 80 yards away from each other. I saw Poppa put his right hand up until the seal quit looking around and put his head on the ice. After watching the seal for a little while, Poppa scooted a little closer. I could see the mist from the open water in front of the seal. The seal would put his head on the ice and sleep in snatches, then look around, smelling the air, at the same time alert for any danger, but enjoying the rest on the ice with the sunshine warming everything.

The hole was to the left of the seal and the big seal was laying with the tail pointing north. Poppa came from the east, and soon I noticed he was not going straight for the seal, but for the waterhole.

Poppa stopped about five yards away from the big seal and untied the line attached to his harpoon. He concentrated on the open water, not wanting the seal to feel threatened by anything he did. He mimicked the movements of the seal so well that he was laying 15 feet away from the big seal. He watched as the seal closed his eyes and he counted to 20, then sat up. He aimed his harpoon at the seal and took three quick steps before hurling the harpoon at the sleeping seal.

The harpoon went in just behind the left front flipper and into the heart. The big seal jumped when the harpoon hit, then plopped down dead. Poppa held the rawhide rope attached to the harpoon, yanking it once to stop the big seal's heart.

I climbed down from the ridge and pulled the sled over and started running to Poppa. While I was running, I saw Poppa put some snow in his mouth. Then a little while later, he opened the seal's mouth and let the melted snow water trickle down into the seal's mouth. When he got done, he closed the seal's mouth and started to cut his harpoon out of the seal carcass with his hunting knife.

When I got closer, I could see it was a ringed seal, about eight feet long. Poppa cut a little hole on the stomach and we pulled out the intestines. We cleaned out the long intestines with fresh water that had melted and made a little pond about six feet in diameter.

After we cleaned the intestines, Poppa braided it, using a single braid. He then stuffed it back into the stomach of the seal. He then made holes on both sides of the cut and weaved a rawhide rope through and tied it shut.

We put the seal on the sled and pulled it back to camp. He had harpooned the seal about a hundred yards out on the ice, straight out from the tent. There were two ridges we had to pull the 350 pound seal over. I pulled the rope in front while poppa pushed the sled from behind.

When we got to the top of the second ridge, Poppa took out the two harpoons and his float hook. He put those aside and had me leave my rifle there. We then pulled the Ringed seal to camp and put it down in the cellar, alongside of the bags of trout fish.

"Did you watch everything I did while going after that seal?" asked Poppa as we walked back to the first ridge, pulling the empty sled.

"Yes, it was like watching two seals on the ice," I said as we climbed the ridge and stopped by our rifles.

Poppa pulled out his flask and we both had a drink of water. He tied the harpoons on the sled and we put our rifles over our right shoulders and started walking out on the ice. After climbing over several ridges, we stopped on the top of one overlooking a large flat area with seals sleeping on the ice.

Poppa untied the shorter harpoon. It was the same one he used on the Ringed seal. He took my rifle and gave me the harpoon. He then started untying the pieces of Polar bear skin from his leg and left arm.

He had me lift my left arm up and he tied one piece on my left leg. The piece went from below my left knee up under my left elbow. After he tied that on, he tied the other piece of Polar bear skin on my left arm.

I could still use my left arm and Poppa handed me the harpoon. He took the wooden tip guard off before he sat down and fixed his binoculars around his neck. He made sure his rifle was close at hand. He pointed at two seals and without saying a word I took the harpoon in my right and held it down low. I then slowly started walking just a little left of the first one. That would put the second seal in line with the first.

I was about 150 yards away when I lay down on my left side. The Polar bear skins tied on my left leg and arm kept me dry and made sliding across the snow and ice very easy.

I moved across the ice with the whole length of my body showing to the seal. I mimicked the movements of a seal, putting my mittened right hand up for a while, then moving closer to the seal. First, I would move my legs forward and put the harpoon in front, then moved my middle. Inch by inch I pushed the harpoon. The tip was covered with white cloth.

I was almost 50 yards away from the seal when a flock of Eider ducks flew overhead. I lifted my right mitten up, hoping the seal would think another seal was looking up at the flying ducks.

When the other seal finally put it's head down on the ice, I put my arm down and counted to ten before I scooted forward three yards.

I stopped when the near seal moved a front flipper. The seal soon stopped moving and I scooted forward another foot.

I patiently put the harpoon in front before moving the middle of my body forward. When one or the other seal moved, I just lay there in full view of the closer one. Soon I could see the closer one was a young Bearded seal and the next one over was a Spotted seal. The closer one was twice as heavy as the smaller Spotted seal.

As I got closer, I could smell the seal. I saw the hole in the ice about two feet in front of the Bearded seal. I inched my way closer and closer. I figured the seal to be about nine feet long. It looked so much bigger when up close. I'm five feet tall, so it would be four feet longer than me. I smiled and moved a little closer.

When I was five yards away I thought about standing up and running close enough to throw the harpoon but the big seal put his head up and looked around.

After looking around, the big seal put his head back on the ice. I counted to 20 then scooted a little closer to the seal. I was about ten feet away when the smaller seal put his head up and looked around. It smelled the air and made sure there was no danger before it lay it's head down too.

I slowly sat up and took the cloth away from the tip of the harpoon. I stood up and took a step closer before I threw the harpoon into the side of the big seal. My aim was true and I quickly yanked on the line. The harpoon hit the seal's heart and when I jerked on the line, it fell on the ice, dead.

I caught movement from the corner of my eye and could see the other seal had no place to go. The bigger seal had come up later, and the other smaller seal had just scooted over. It tried to get away, but had no hole to dive into.

I looked at the big seal and saw it was dead. I pulled on the line, but the tip of the harpoon was firmly embedded in the big seal and it would take too long to cut it out. I dropped the line and pulled my hunting knife out.

Holding my knife, I ran after the spotted seal. I caught up with it about 20 yards away from the big seal. I jumped on the back and stabbed the seal. When the seal quit moving, I stood up and looked towards Poppa. I then cleaned my knife by stabbing it into the snow.

I scooped some snow and put some in my mouth. When it melted, I opened the dead seal's mouth and let some fresh water drip into it. Then I walked quickly over to the big seal and did the same. Only after the seals had fresh water did I look at Poppa as he came over the ice pulling the sled. He had his rifle slung over one shoulder on a strap.

He started running towards me. I could see the harpoon on the sled as it bounced along behind Poppa. He had tied my rifle on the sled and I thought it would tip over. He ran like he was a teenager, holding the line with one hand and his other hand was on his bouncing rifle. He had shiny white teeth with a dark sun and wind burned face, and was covered in his white hunting coat.

He had waterproof seal skin mukluks that went up just above his knees and his white hunting coat had a hood and an extra large pocket in front with a flap covering the zipper. The zipper ran the length of his chest and the pocket was on the inside of the pullover hunting coat.

Soon he was by my side and he gave me a big hug.

"You did it son. I watched every move and when the spotted seal started across the ice, I knew you were by the only hole in the ice. You made me so proud when I saw you give them fresh water!" Poppa said as he held my shoulders and looked into my eyes.

We both smiled and he started untying the two pieces of Polar bear hide on my left side. When they were both off, he rolled them up and tied them on the sled.

While he was doing that I cut the belly of the nine-foot seal, and grabbing ahold of the intestine, I took off running across the ice. I ran about 50 feet before the intestines quit coming out of the Bearded seal. Poppa cut the intestines and moved the cut ends about 30 feet away. I then started cleaning the long intestines.

I must have used two or three gallons of water to clean the intestines. I just stood there with a cup and poured the water down the long intestine until the water came out clean from the other end. After I poured in six cups I would follow the intestines 30 feet over, then come back lifting the guts along the way. I kept doing that until the water came out clear and clean.

I then did a single braid and made the long intestines easier to carry. I shoved it back into the stomach and made holes across from each other on the stomach of the nine foot long bearded seal.

I then tied a rawhide string and closed the two-foot long cut on the belly of the seal. I cut one place on the front flipper and go an extra long rawhide rope and tied the end on the flipper.

We then slid the rope under the seal from the head until it was at the flipper. We did that four times, then pulled the line and rolled the big 800 pound seal up an ice ramp and into the sled. The tail dragged a little, but all the seal's weight was on the sled.

While I was working on the intestines, Poppa had attached a line to the spotted seal. He cut a hole under the jaw of the seal all the way through the tongue. He put the line through the hole and pulled it up around the nose and back through the hole.

He let out about 10 feet, then made a loop. He then put on a head strap that was about three inches wide and fits his forehead. He would pull the weight of the seal using his head, that way he had both of his hands free, while pulling the spotted seal over the ice and snow.

We both put our rifles (still unfired) over our shoulders. The harpoons were tied on the sled and we were ready to go.

We walked side by side. I pulled the sled with the bearded seal, while Poppa pulled the spotted seal. When we got to the first ridge, Poppa just took the strap off his head and pushed the sled while I pulled the rope in front.

First, I climbed the ridge and started pulling. The rope was around my right shoulder and Poppa pushed while I pulled the rope, using my leg muscles. We slowly pushed the sled over the top of the ridge, then Poppa went back for the smaller spotted seal.

It didn't take Poppa long to go down and put the strap on his forehead, then hurry up the ridge. He used his hands and feet, and when he reached the top he stopped and pulled the spotted seal over it. He took the head strap off and we worked together to get the big bearded seal down the other side of the ridge. After we got it down, I went back up and got the smaller seal.

When I got down, we walked side by side. Poppa pulled the sled and I pulled the spotted seal. We went like that until we reached the next ridge and worked together on the big heavy seal.

When we went over the last ridge we walked the rest of the way to camp. We pulled the two seals over by the underground cellar and put them close by. We untied the bearded seal from the sled and tipped the sled to deposit the load.

Our dogs barked and barked. They were eager to go, but we decided it would be easier to travel over land after the snow on the trail got harder. When the sun warmed the land, a lot of moisture went up in the air. At night it often got foggy in the spring, but it cooled off enough to make the snow on the ground firm enough to travel on.

We fed the dogs, then loaded our shotguns and walked up side the hill and enjoyed the day. It was around nine a.m. and we had a whole day to relax. We ate sandwiches and drank hot coffee from the thermos. Before we finished our sandwiches, a flock of geese came flying alongside of the hill. We shot together and a half a dozen fell.

I ran down and chased the wounded one until I caught up with it and wrung it's neck. I collected all six and tied them two apiece and slung them over my shoulder, and I carried them to the trail going home and set them down. I covered them with grass and willows before going back up the hill to Poppa.

"You should have brought your .22, then you wouldn't have to run so much." said Poppa as a big smile lit his face.

"I should've listened to you when you told me to bring it." I replied as I picked up my shotgun and put another #4 shell in the chamber.

I picked up my half-eaten sandwich and looked south where the geese were coming from. I took a bite and drank my coffee. My coffee was lukewarm, but strong, after leaving it sit while I chased the geese.

Poppa picked up his binoculars and looked down south. He adjusted the sight as he looked along the coast. The Arctic Ocean was west and the end of the Brooks Range Mountains ended here. He smiled while he was looking, then put the Bushnell binoculars down.

"There is a flock of big honkers coming, about the fifth flock back. We will let these other geese fly by and wait for them, OK?" He said.

I chewed on my bite of sandwich and nodded, smiling.

Poppa had an old double barrel shotgun. Someone had sawed about a foot off the front. This .12 gauge was deadly at close range. He had another one he carried when geese hunting. It was called "Long Tom"and had a 36 inch barrel, with a choke in front, a bolt action .12 gauge single shot.

I had a Remington .12 gauge pump, which I took the spacer off so it would hold a couple more shots. Using 2-3/4 inch #4s, I could have one in the barrel and four in the chamber.

I finished my sandwich and put my cup back on the thermos. After screwing it tight, I put the thermos back into the caribou skin pouch and tied it shut. I quit moving when a flock of yellow legs flew by.

We watched as the flock came closer and closer. We had watched from below and picked this spot. We had seen a few flocks go by while still below the hill. We picked a place where there was tall grass and made sure it was on the level where the geese are flying.

When the flock of yellow-legged geese flew by, the closest was ten feet away. They flew in a line and we would have knocked down more than one if we wanted, but we were waiting for those honkers.

The geese let out gentle clucking sounds to each other as they traveled the invisible highway. Their powerful wings all flapped in a slow but sure pace. Each goose was going the way many, many others had flown year in and year out. Millions of ducks, geese, and many birds migrated north every year.

"When those honkers come, I want you to shoot at the ones flying far on the outside. I will use this short gun for the close ones," said Poppa.

"OK," I said, as we watched another flock of geese coming in the air flying along, straight for us.

We watched three more flocks go by. One flock had about a hundred yellow legs flying in formation, headed north. In an awesome line, they cruised by looking at each other while clucking in low, almost silent communication. The wind from their wings moved my hair, then they were flying away from us, headed north to their nesting grounds.

When the honkers came, we were ready. I made sure there was a live round in the barrel and when they came closer, I moved to Poppa's right. We followed the big honkers with our shotguns. I aimed four feet in front of the geese, knowing when and where the #4's would hit. I planned to hit four that were in a tight bunch. Then, my next shot I would shoot about a foot in front of any Poppa didn't shoot.

That is exactly what happened when the flock of big honkers came. We knocked down nine with the two shots we each had fired. I ran after three wounded ones and soon put nine big honkers under the grass and willows, with the six yellow legs.

Poppa and I hunted for about an hour before we decided we had a load to bring home. We shot 68 geese. Some were yellow legs, Canadian, Canadian honkers, and snow geese. We filled four big gunny sacks with geese and put them on our little sled, after I took all the willows off. We had hidden the sled before climbing the side of the ridge.

Poppa used his head strap. He tied it on the ring where my line was attached. We carried our shotguns as we followed the snow on the bottom of the ridge. When we got on the trail, we had an easier time pulling the sled. It was warm and we both took our white hunting coats off and tied them on the sled. Soon we were back at camp and we put the bags of geese by the two seals.

The underground cellar had snow covering it, about a foot deep. We had used a handsaw to cut the snow away from the cellar door. The door opened on rawhide hinges and was made from seasoned wood. There was a layer of topsoil that had to be removed when first opening of the season. It was put back on top after the last hunt in the fall. We had to make sure no heat would melt the permafrost that our cellar was dug into. It was four feet by four feet and had a ladder lead straight into the middle of a 10 by 12 room. The dog food was on one side and the food for the family was on the other side of the ladder.

Poppa hitched four dogs in harness and had them pull the Ringed Seal he had sneaked up on and killed with the harpoon. He put that on my sled, along with the two bags of geese. He tied them in a tarp, then he filled his sled.

His sled was bigger and we put the big Bearded Seal alongside of the spotted seal. He put our grub box way in the back and after making sandwiches, he put them in the pouch hanging between his handlebars where he could reach them. He put our thermos full of hot, strong coffee in the caribou skin cover in along with some extra thin rawhide line for general purposes. He put the other two gunny sacks of geese in and last he put dog food in front, outside of the tarp. The dog food was two gunny sacks full of white fish from the late fall.

We tied everything down and attached our hunting pouches on the side of the sleds. We put our rifles in and zipped them shut.

When everything was all tied down and ready to go, we wandered around looking for any trash, and left everything just the way it was before we got here.

When we did everything we could possibly do, we loosened all the dogs. We let them run free while we gathered the two chains we used to tie them down. Our harnesses were laid out in front of both sleds and Poppa called his leader. He put the big gray dog in harness and scratched behind his ears.

"Hold them here, Howler," Poppa said and he walked to the sled and called his wheel dogs. He called each dog by name and they came to his call. He worked back up to his leader, putting a dog in harness until he had all nine ready to go.

I did the same and I couldn't help smiling when I put the harness on my last one. Poppa had one dog run loose who would let us know if there was anything along the trail we should know about. His loose running dog, Poppa called "Matches."

When we travel with a lot of meat he would let his long-legged Alaskan husky run loose and watch for danger. He controlled the free-running dog with whistles done by mouth.

One long piercing whistle would have the dog run ahead. Matches quickly raced ahead until Poppa let out two short whistles. When Matches heard two short ones, he would keep looking back so he could match the pace of the two teams. Three quick whistles and Matches would come bounding back to Poppa.

Sometimes it was awesome to watch Poppa and Matches communicate with each other. When Poppa gave the right answer Matches would wag his tail so hard he would almost loose his balance. He let Poppa know everything along the trail and we traveled slow together, saving the strength of my young dogs as we climbed up the trail. It was very steep at one place and we made it by going up at an angle. After passing that one steep place, the trail went upward, but not so steep. When we topped the ridge we stopped the two dog teams and looked at the Noatak River.

The town of Noatak was 12 miles away and the air was so clear we could see the roof tops. We had a cup of hot coffee and ate a sandwich while we let the dogs rest from the climb from the ocean camp. From here on, it would be easy going. All down hill and with a good covering of hard-packed snow.

We could see most of the trail as it slowly zigzagged east until it hit the river. Then it followed the river bend the rest of the way upriver to the village. We could see the spruce trees all along the river. The river ran between the mountain range.

Way off to the southeast was a large herd of caribou. The huge gathering of caribou made the land on the other side of the river come alive with activity. The caribou were migrating across the tundra, making a thousand mile journey every year.

We saw several dog teams leave the village and head down river to wait for the massive herd to cross the river.

We decided it was a perfect time to go to the country cache and leave our load and go after caribou with everyone. That's what we do to survive through the harsh Arctic winters. We smiled at each other.

The End

FAMILY HUNTING CAMP

By Wendell Amisimak Stalker

May 5, 2017

This is a work of fiction. Names, characters, places and incidents are either the product of the author's imagination or are used fictitiously, and any resemblance to actual persons, living or dead, business establishments, events or locales is entirely coincidental.

"Come gee," my father, Auk, said in a loud voice. He then gave a loud piercing whistle, he clapped his hands together a couple times, and again hollered, "Come, gee."

I lifted myself from the snow and watched the runaway dog team make a sharp turn to the right, and started back toward us. My name is Quaq and I had just been thrown off the back of the sled the dogs were pulling. I had hit a bump on the trail and had been dragged for a little while before letting go of the sled. The only thing hurt was my young pride.

My father walked to the trail and stopped the dog team. He reached out to his leader and said, "Good dog, Avu, good boy!" By then I had dusted the snow off and walked up to him.

"You OK?" he asked with a smile on his face.

"I hang on alright, but had to let go." I walked to the sled and he let the lead dog go.

I told the dog team to start and got them turned around. I was taking a load of Shii-fish to our camp about a mile away from where we were fishing. My right elbow was a little sore, first from pulling up Shii-fish, then being pulled by the dog team. Some of the fish were longer than four feet, and this was my third trip.

As the dogs pulled the sled, I could hear the sled runners whisper a soft gentle crackle. I moved to the right runner and looked past the huge load of fish, then watched as the dogs pulled me onto the main river. As we turned, I could see our log cabin.

The cabin was a simple little place we used when hunting and fishing. It was up the side of the riverbank, far enough to escape the annual spring flood. Though sometimes when the ice piled up downstream, it would flood the cabin. When you go into the cabin you could see a line about five feet up the wall.

The dogs turned off the river and started climbing up the side of the bank. I got them to get close to our pile of fish and stopped. I put the brake down and made sure it was secure. I tied my mittens behind my back and untied the rope holding the fish. It was a good feeling to know our family would have good Shii-fish to eat. I took the rope off and started to move the fish from the sled. The pile of fish there was about a third of all the fish my father, Auk, and I had caught.

After putting all the fish on the pile, I threw the tarp over and put the pieces of wood on to keep it from blowing away. I walked to the back of the sled and got the dog team going back on the trail. As I was starting to go towards Auk, I heard a shot.

The dogs picked up speed as we went downriver. We turned into the slough where I had left Auk and saw a big moose come out of the willows. Then Auk shot again and the big moose fell.

I drove the dog team over to Auk and saw him walk to the moose, pointing the gun at it. He walked up to the moose and touched it with his foot. When the moose didn't move, I saw Auk take the shell out of the chamber. He then looked at me and waived. It didn't take me very long to reach him because the dogs knew Auk had shot something and they would get to eat. I put the breaks on and told the dogs to stop. After I put the break hook down, I walked to Auk and the big moose.

"Look there, he have only one big antler," he said as I got closer. "No wonder it was making such a racket there in the willows. I think he was trying to take the antler off."

Auk reached down and put some clean snow in his mouth, then he opened the mouth of the moose and let the water drip into it. He then put his rifle down and pulled out his hunting knife.

Working together, we skinned the big moose and cut it into manageable pieces. We put the meat on the sled and strapped everything down. The big moose made a load all by itself. We even took the head with one antler.

As we worked on the moose, my father told me how he had heard the unknown making more and more noise in the near riverbank. He said he took out his .45 caliber revolver and looked. Then he walked to our pile of hunting gear and got his big rifle. He laughed a little when he told me of loading the .12 gauge shotgun with slug shots. He told me to remind him to take out the slugs before he blast a ptarmigan to tiny little pieces. We both laughed and I got on the sled with the moose. Auk picked up the break hook and started the dogs.

We brought the moose meat under the cache. Right under the door. The cache was 10 feet up in the air to keep our meat away from animals. I climbed up the ladder and opened the door. Auk then threw me the rope we had attached to a hindquarter. As I pulled on the rope,

Auk pushed from underneath. We put the meat up and I struggled to move the heavy moose leg away from the door.

We continued to put all the meat up into the cache, keeping enough for a couple meals. We also left the forelegs. Those we put by the cabin. Later we would take the meat off, along with all the muscle membrane. We kept a few empty one-pound cans from Darigold butter. After we cracked the bones, we would put the marrow into the cans and take them home.

The moose was very fat, with about five inches on the back hump. I had to drag the big head, even there was only one antler. I put it in the arctic entryway and went back out. I picked up some snow and used it to clean some of the blood from my clothes.

Auk had turned the dog team around and we started back to our fishing holes. We had seven dogs and soon we could see the pile of fish. Auk had to keep the dogs from going to the moose intestines. We would feed the dogs only after their work was done. Auk had fed each dog just a little when we cut the meat up. We knew the dogs would want to lay down after they ate a full meal.

I jumped off the sled as soon as Auk stopped the dogs. I then started to load the sled with fish. Auk walked to his hole in the ice and stooped down to break the ice that formed in the short time it took to put the moose meat away. It was around 10 degrees below, with no wind.

The ice was three feet thick where we made our fishing holes. We were at our family hunting camp on the Kobuk River. It is located on a tributary off the main river. We had a lookout tower standing up about 40 feet high. The tower had to be over the tall willows.

Even before Auk got done cleaning the ice from his hole, he had put his hook in the water. Almost as soon as he put the hook in, he got a bite. He started pulling up a fish. I could see his hands as the fish tried to get away. He pulled up a Shii-fish that was around three feet long. He threw it onto the ice and the fish spit the hook out.

I could see his face light up with a big smile. He shoved the fish over by the big pile. The fish flopped around a little, then just laid there. Auk checked his bait and line. The bait we used was cut from the bottom of the fish's jaw. We then used tie-wire to make it harder for the fish to steal the bait.

I filled the sled up and tied everything down. As I started the dog team, I could remember watching Auk as he made the fish hooks out of white walrus ivory. First, he clamped the ivory onto his vise and split the ivory, starting from the tip of the tusk. He cut down about five inches, then cut the two pieces off. He quickly rounded off the edges with his file. He clamped one onto the vise and drilled a hole into it about an inch from the wider end of the ivory. That will be for the single barb made from the handle of a five-gallon Blazo can. He used the drill and made a hole through the thinner end, then about an inch back, he put two holes on each side. He then put glue into the two holes and put in baleen, for the eyes. He put in the metal hook after he bent the piece using heat from a Primer stove. He cut a length of baleen and put it through the hole. The baleen was flexible but very tough. He then sanded it until it had a good shine. He used ninety-pound test line and braided about two feet to use as a leader. He tied it onto a wooden handle in the shape of a J.

As I drove the dog team, I listened to the gentle crackling noise the sled runners made. The dogs turned onto the main river and brought me gliding across the snow. I really enjoyed mushing the dogs. The sun was still shining and I knew our dogs were just as happy to pull the sled. I saw a flock of ptarmigan across the river as they landed in the willows. I turned the team and went up to the pile of fish.

I put the break hook down and made sure it was going to hold the team. I pulled the tarp off the pile and untied the line holding the fish on the sled. As I transferred the fish from the sled to the pile, I smiled because there are times when we would not even get one bite, no matter how long we jigged our hooks.

After unloading the fish, I made sure the break hook was still secure, then walked to the cabin. I went in and quickly made a fire in the wood stove. I filled the kettle with ice and put the pot of caribou soup on one edge to warm up. I then went back to the sled and got the dog team headed back to Auk.

When I got back, I turned the dog team over by some willows and stopped. I set the break hook and, taking a length of rope, I walked to the lead dog, Avu, and tied the rope onto the main line. Then I tied the rope to a willow. That way the dogs wouldn't bunch up and get tangled.

I walked over to Auk and smiled as he pushed another fish to the pile. I picked up my hook and broke the ice on my fishing hole using a hatchet. I scooped the ice out and unraveled the fishing line. I checked my bait and put the hook in the water.

I told Auk I had made a fire at the cabin and started to heat up the leftover soup. He said, "That's good, I just started getting hungry."

"I, ah...oh my," I said just when a fish bit my hook. It yanked the wooden jigger down until the ice stopped it from going down any further. It had hit so hard it made my wrist sting, but I hung onto my stick.

Auk was looking at me as I was telling him about making the soup warm. He knew I had a big fish by the way my jigging stick was jerked down in a violent tug.

At first I tried to pull the fish up like we do with smaller fish, but it was too tough. Every time I pulled up, it would pull my hands back down. I straightened my back and wrapped the line around my mittens and pulled, using only my legs. When I stood up straight, I quickly wrapped more line as I bent my legs. I just made sure I didn't give the fish any slack. I slowly pulled the fish up and when I got the head started up in the ice hole, the water started overflowing onto the ice. The fish was so big around that the water in the three-foot thick ice hole had nowhere else to go but onto the ice. Soon there was water everywhere around my fishing hole. I looked down and saw the big fish close his mouth. Every time the fish closed his mouth, water came gushing onto the ice. The auger we used was 12 inches wide, being the widest they had in the store.

I finally got the head above the water and, taking off one mitten, I grabbed a hold of the gills. I held it there while I shook my other mitten off and, holding the fish by the gills, I straightened my legs and pulled the giant Shii-fish up. I am five feet and three inches tall and when I lifted the fish up, the head was level with mine, but the tail was still in the water.

I then threw it off to the side and it started flopping around on the ice. I didn't know when Auk walked by my side until he told me to go wipe my mukluks on the snow before the water seep in and freeze.

I quickly walked away from my fishing hole and proceeded to take all the moisture off my mukluks using snow. It didn't take long and I walked back. Auk was saying, "Yoi, yoi," as he took the hook out of the fish's mouth.

I rubbed my wrist and smiled really big. I knew nobody would believe me but there was the big Shii-fish. It was the biggest Shii-fish I had ever seen and just think, it really did bite my hook.

My father, Auk, had taught me good how to fish. We used a bright and shiny ivory hook to get their attention, we put on fresh bait the fish could taste. I tap my wooden jigging stick because to the big fish, it sounded like a wounded fish. We used extra strong fishing line, and we moved around looking for the fish. Many times we made our fishing holes downstream of a tree or something stuck to the river bottom. The fish would bunch up behind things like that so they didn't have to fight the river currents.

There was a tree under water about three feet upstream where we made our holes through the ice when we started that morning after spending the night in the hunting cabin. It was kind of slow, but after we caught a couple, the movement of the fish trying to get off our hooks had attracted other fish. That is why we caught so many that day.

The slough we fished had been fished by our grandfathers. The building of the log cabin had been done by Auk and his relatives. That was our family hunting and fishing ground.

I had fished there all my life, but that was the biggest one I caught so far. We fished for another hour before the fish slowed down biting. We loaded up the sled so full that Auk had me stand in the back with him. I stood on the left side and when Auk pulled the brake hook out we both pushed so it would be easier for the dogs to gain momentum. Once we got started good, Auk and I had our own different view because the pile of fish was so high on the sled, I had to lean off to the side just to see the dogs.

We turned onto the main river and I saw the flock of ptarmigan that had landed there. Some were perched up in the willows and some were on the snow. I remembered how tasty they are and thought about taking a walk with the shot gun. It would be good if I could sneak up on them and see how many I could get with one shot. We had bird shot, number twos, and slugs for the .12 gauge shotgun.

We helped push the loaded sled up the riverbank and stopped by the pile of fish. Auk set the break hook and I removed the tarp off the big pile of Shii-fish. Auk untied the rope and we unloaded the sled. Auk and I unhooked the dogs and, one at a time, we tied them to their poles. Each dog had a plywood house with grass inside.

We gave each dog a piece of half-dried salmon, and I started cooking for them. I put water in the half of a 55-gallon drum we had converted into a huge cooking pot. The other half of the drum was fixed into a fireplace. I made a fire and put the bucket of moose intestines we had brought for the dogs in, along with a few strips of seal blubber. I made sure the fire was going good under the cooking pot, then I went into the cabin. I went out once in a while to stir the dog food.

Auk had put another piece of wood in the stove and I took my warm parka off. The caribou soup on the side of the stove had thawed and it didn't take very long to heat it up a little quicker by putting the pot closer to the stovepipe.

That soup was starting to smell really good. Auk went to his grub box and pulled out two plates and two bowls. As he straightened up, our dogs all started barking. Auk put the bowls down and walked to the door. He opened the door with his right hand and put his left by his rifle.

He threw the door open and stepped out. He waived to someone out on the dog team trail.

He hollered, "Hi, Savik. Welcome!"

I saw Uncle Savik (behind his team of dogs) smiling as he mushed the dogs alongside of the cabin. He set his break hook and pointed at the pile of Shii-fish as he walked to his brother. He took his mitten off and shook hands with Auk and gave me a big bear hug.

The skins moved and my cousin, Liq, poked his head out and smiled.

"Hi, Cuz. Welcome to camp!" I said as I ran to him.

Savik laughed and said, "He had a warm trip from town!"

Liq gave me a hand shake and jumped out of the sled. He walked to Auk and gave him a hug. Liq and I were born the same month, he was 10 days older.

We helped them tie the dogs up behind the cabin. I put some more water in the cooking dog food and I added a half dozen Shii-fish. Liq and I cut the fish with our hatchet. I put in a few more strips of old seal blubber and put more wood and stoked the fire. I stirred everything with an old wooden paddle. We put the lid on and walked to the cabin.

Auk and Savik had set the table with bowls for everyone. We took off our mittens and parkas. We rushed to the table and sat down. Savik smiled and said, "There is a wash basin on that table in the corner, feel free to clean the scales off nephew."

We laughed and Liq and I both washed our hands. The smell of the caribou soup made us clean up really fast and soon we joined the men and had a great meal.

We all got big bowls of caribou soup and the homemade donuts were a huge hit, and tundra tea by the gallons. We had a plate to cut the caribou meat on. We used seal oil for a dip. I put Worchestershire Sauce and a little touch of Tabasco and some salt into the seal oil. We cut a piece of meat and dipped it into the seal oil to add more nutrients.

We all had second helpings of caribou soup and had a bowl of salmon berries with a little sugar sprinkled on top and a touch of canned milk.

After Liq and I washed the dishes, we went out and put dog food into their food bowls. The soup cooled off in the bowls and by the time I had filled the last bowl, the ones we filled first were cold. Liq helped by moving the bowls after I filled them. We waited a few minutes, then started giving all the dogs a bowl of soup. We put the empty cooking pot upside down and went into the cabin.

Savik smiled and asked us to bring in the moose head. Liq and I turned around and went to the moose head. I grabbed a hold of one ear and the bottom of the big nose. Liq took a firm grip of the antler and we lifted the head up. I walked backwards and we put the head on a piece of cardboard.

"The neck must have been pretty sore on that moose!" said Auk as he pointed at the big antler.

Savik shook the moose head holding it by the antler. He set it down and Auk grabbed an ear and put his knee on the nose. Savik tried, but the antler wouldn't come off. Auk reached for the hatchet and, using the blunt end, he hit the base of the antler. After hitting it a few times, he held it down and Savik slowly removed the antler.

The base of the antler was bloody, so Savik put it back in the arctic entryway. Auk started skinning the big head. Savik came back in with two legs and I went out and brought in the other two. The moose forelegs were heavy.

We put down another piece of card board and set the moose legs on it. Savik and I cut the meat off the forelegs while Liq helped Auk skin the head.

Savik put some water into a big pot and put it on the wood stove. As we cut a piece of meat we put it in the pot. Soon we had all the meat in the cooking pot. We scraped the muscle membrane off the leg bones and hit the bone with the back of our knives. We extracted the marrow and put it in one pound cans.

Auk and Liq quickly skinned the moose head and we put the head back in the arctic entry way wrapped in the cardboard we had used on the floor.

Auk put fuel into the Coleman lantern while it was still bright enough to see. Then put it on the table and started pumping it. The lantern had to be filled with air so there would be pressure enough to send the fuel up to the mantel. After it was pumped full of air, he put a match to it and the little cabin was bright as day.

I went out to the fish pile and poked the fish until I found one that was not frozen. When I brought the fish in, I put it in our tub and set it closer to the wood stove. I wanted it to thaw out good so I could cut it.

"How come you didn't bring in your big one?" asked Savik smiling.

"I'm going to give that one to grandma Pook-ak. I told Auk earlier," I said as I took my knife out and got the sharpening stone out of the grub box. I sat down at the table and put an edge on my hunting knife, then pulled the tub closer. I put a piece of plastic on the floor and starting cutting the fish around the gills. After I cut on both sides of the gills to the bone, I cut along the top, following the back. After I cut the skin all the way to the tail, I followed the backbone and took the flesh off with the skin. I turned the fish over and did the same with the other side. When I got done, I had all the flesh in one piece, with the skin still on. I cut the head off and took the gills off. I cut the stomach open and scraped the little fish out. The Shii-fish had four small trout inside. I took the liver and eggs out and put them in water with the stomach and washed them. I then put them into a Ziploc bag. I put the head into another bag, and set it aside. I wrapped the flesh with the skin still on in the plastic and put everything on a shelf in the arctic entry way. I cut the little fish I had taken out of the stomach into small pieces, along with the gills. We would pour that into our fishing holes to attract more fish.

As I was doing all that, Auk and I told Savik and Liq about catching the big fish and Auk told us about hearing something making loud noise in the willows and how he shot the big moose that had only one antler.

Savik and Liq listened to us and would ask a question once in a while. Savik made it hot in the little cabin as he cooked the moose meat. The muscle on the forelegs took a long time to cook. He threw in some salt. He added hot water from the kettle as it evaporated down. The smell of cooking meat filled the little cabin.

After Auk and I told our stories, Savik talked about their trip from town. He said, "I saw five hundred musk-oxen on the trail and Liq didn't even know!"

"No way, I didn't go to sleep. I would have seen them, too!" said Liq. "He is just pulling your leg. We saw a couple flocks of ptarmigan, but no musk-oxen."

Savik laughed and said, "I thought you were sleeping because the caribou skin you were in didn't move!"

We all laughed and the early evening passed. We were just in our t-shirts because of the cooking. The dogs outside were quiet and the stars were out. There was a full moon and the Northern Lights danced across the sky.

Liq asked his uncle, Auk, if he could tell a story. "Please Uncle, tell us a hunting story. I want to hear about hunting out in the ocean!"

"Yes, brother, tell us about hunting with the people up north. You know about using an umiaq." said Savik smiling at Auk.

I put another piece of wood in the stove and made sure there was a lot of water in the kettle. I removed all the bowls and plates, checked the teapot, and added more sugar into the bowl.

Auk cleared his throat and had one last bite of his donut. He drank it down with tundra tea.

"I will tell you about a scary walrus hunt we had out in the ocean." Auk said as he made himself comfortable.

"It was in the spring and we had been out on the ice a few hours when we saw a herd of walrus. The walrus were swimming along the edge of the ice. Our skin boat was there by the edge, ready to push out if a whale came by. A huge male walrus jumped upon the ice and made it's way towards our skin boat. I threw a harpoon and got it just behind the right flipper. The huge walrus didn't stop. Even everyone with a rifle was shooting at it. It dragged the boat a little ways before finally stopping on the ice. Our skin boat had a hole where the tusk had gone through. We had not even put the boat in the water and we had to sew the hole shut. The wooden frame was not damaged. We moved the skin boat away from the water and Qonaqpuk took his sewing kit out and started sewing the hole. The first thing he did was make the skin around the hole wet. He kept splashing water on the skin until it was soaked and pliable. He cut another piece for the plug and carefully sewed the hole shut.

I watched him for a little while, then went to the walrus. He put a rope around the front and back and wrapped it a few times. Then we pulled the ropes and rolled the huge walrus away from the edge of the water.

As we were sharpening our knives, I looked at the harpoon sticking out of the walrus Someone behind me hollered and I turned around. I saw an even bigger walrus already half out of the water. I ran with the other hunters to our guns. We only had knives.

The big walrus went straight for the dead walrus. I was surprised at how fast an animal that big could move across the ice. I could see the redness of his eyes as he reached the dead walrus. It grabbed the dead walrus under the flipper and, using his right (just like a person would hold someone to help them walk), the big male walrus started dragging the dead one towards the open water.

The water was about thirty yards away when someone fired the first shot. I grabbed my 30:06 and quickly loaded the chamber. I took a few steps off to the side and sighted right behind the ear. I squeezed the trigger and hit the walrus where I aimed. The harpoon line had been laying in a pile near the dead walrus. We had not cut it out yet and Avatuqpuq (the grandson of Qonaqpuk) was being pulled out to sea. The line was wrapped around his left ankle and he emptied his rifle as the big bull walrus dragged the dead walrus (the harpoon and line were both designed not to break).

When the big walrus didn't stop, I ran as fast as I could and caught up with the walrus. I ran a few steps and pointed my rifle just above the eye. The end of my rifle was about four inches away when I pulled the trigger. The big walrus finally came to a stop, just about four yards away from the water. I quickly put another shell into my gun. There were a couple more shots fired before we all slowly walked to the two walrus.

I went to Avatuqpuq and untangled the line and helped him up to his feet. He was still holding his rifle and his hands shook a little when he saw how close the open water was.

"Thank you, guys!" said Avatuqpuq as he was surrounded by all the hunters.

Qonaqpuk gave his grandson a hug and wiped the tears from his eyes. "I really thought that crazy walrus was going to take you away from me son," he said as he hugged his grandson again.

I walked to the edge of the ice and stood there for a while. I knew it was a mile or more deep there. As I was looking down into the water, I knew there was no way we could have helped Avatuqpuq once the big walrus started sinking. I thought how an animal would give his own life to save one of their own. I pulled out my .45 cal. revolver and emptied it into the water. I knew the concussion would chase the other walrus away.

We took turns cutting and sharpening until both walrus were cut up. We cut the skin, blubber and meat all the way down to the bone. After we cut a square piece (about 2-1/2 feet by 2-1/2 feet) we would follow the bone and pull the big piece off using gaff hooks.

It took everyone to cut through the skin and blubber. Our knife would be sharp enough to cut only for about six cutting slices, then you have to exchange knives with someone who sharpened the second one. One person is always sharpening, while another is always cutting. Other people holding gaff hooks would move the cut pieces and two other people would make holes all the way around the skin. Once the holes were made all the way around, they would put a rawhide line through and enclose the meat and blubber within it's own skin. It was the sharpening that kept us going smoothly.

The skin of the walrus is a quarter inch thick. Then attached to the skin is a layer of muscle (like hard rubber) about two inches thick, then blubber about six inches thick. The meat is the easiest to cut. Each walrus gave us around a thousand pounds apiece.

I kept one head with tusks and Qonaqpuk kept the other head. Qonaqpuk and I worked together and we turned the stomachs inside out. Both stomachs were full of clams. We washed the ones that still had a shell and filled two five-gallon cans with clams. We took both stomachs and put them on the sled. We would use the stomachs to make drums. We also had flippers, which is an Eskimo delicacy. Qonaqpuk and I have the loudest sound when we play our drums with other drummers.

That was the first day out on the ice waiting alongside an open lead. We caught 30 Beluga whale one day. We finally caught a Bowhead whale that was 45 feet long, but I will always remember when the two big walrus bulls came up on the ice and almost took Avatuqpuq away."

Liq and I made our beds on the floor while Auk and Savik used the beds. We fixed our bed over a huge grizzly bear hide. Before I went to bed, I made sure there was kindling and firewood ready for morning. We banked the fire in the stove and after everyone was in bed, Auk turned the lantern off and it got dark. I listened to Auk as he made his way to his bed in the dark. He shuffled around a little, then got quiet.

The next thing I knew it was already time for me to jump out of bed and quickly make a fire. As soon as I got the fire going and the kettle in place, I jumped back into my blankets.

Liq giggled as I curled up in a fetal position. Soon Auk and Savik got up and started cooking breakfast. Savik put the sourdough for our pancakes over by the stove to thaw out. Auk went to the grub box and pulled out a slab of bacon and his knife. We carried them to the table and, using a cutting board, he started cutting slices off. He put the frying pan on the Primer stove and moved the kettle from the wood stove. He put it on the second burner. The Coleman two-burner heated up the little cabin and we could smell the pancakes and bacon cooking.

Liq and I got up and dressed. When the kettle started boiling, I put some water into our coffee pot and added some coffee. I turned the heat down a little on the second burner and put the coffee pot on the edge of the flame.

While the breakfast was cooking, the older men talked about what they were going to do that day. Liq and I moved aside and watched as Savik turned a pancake over and, using the same spatula, he turned the bacon over and pushed it down on the cast iron frying pan. It was about 15 inches around (without the six inch handle) and Savik cooked the bacon on one side and a pancake on the other.

"The fish were biting all day yesterday until around three in the afternoon," said Auk as he put another plate on the table.

"I had to help my daughter get on the plane yesterday," said Savik. "We came as soon as she got on. She went to Selawik for their school graduation."

"I hope the fish are biting today. I would like to get more Shii-fish," said Auk.

"Yes, brother, I wouldn't mind pulling up a few fish myself," said Savik.

"We will all go to the fishing holes and see if the fish will bite today and if they are biting, I think you and I should fish while the boys take a load of fish to town," said Auk as he smiled at Liq and I.

"That sounds good to me!" said Savik as he took the last pancake off the frying pan. He then put the stack of pancakes on the table.

We ate a good breakfast that I could barely remember because Liq and I were so excited. We dressed in our warm clothes and went out. The sun was shining and it was around five below. There were clouds to the southwest, but they were far away. We started getting the dog team ready. Auk and Savik finished putting everything in order and they too came out. We worked together and quickly got the two teams ready.

I jumped into the sled and Auk pulled the break hook and the dogs started pulling us to the fishing spot about a mile and a half away. It didn't take very long for us to reach the slough and we turned into it.

We saw two wolves eating the moose guts we had left there. Auk pulled the .243 Winchester rifle out of the carry case we had tied alongside of the sled. He put the breaks on and slowed the team so Savik would catch up.

Savik took his rifle out as he got by Auk and both teams got closer. The two wolves were busy eating and Auk and Savik shot at the same time.

Both wolves went down, but I noticed Auk and Savik reloaded as soon as they fired. We were still moving when the willows parted and another wolf came out. The two brothers shot at the same time and the big gray wolf went down, too.

Auk stopped the dog team and walked to the two wolves after he set the brake hook. He pointed his gun at the wolves until he made sure they were not getting up.

Savik did the same to the big gray wolf over by the willows. The snow was deeper off the ice and he had to walk in snow drifts above his knees. He touched the wolf with his rifle, then reached out and started to drag the carcass out.

I ran towards Savik until the deep snow slowed me down. I followed his tracks and when we got together, we grabbed a hold of a hind leg and dragged the big wolf onto the ice. We put the wolf by the other two and noticed how much bigger it was. The wolf was about three feet bigger than the black ones.

"That's good," said Auk. "Our women will have skins for our ruffs."

"Yes, sir. It sure is awesome to get these wolves early in the day," said Savik.

"Look, the wolf is bigger than me," said Liq as he stood there looking at the long wolf lying on the ice.

Auk said, "Those two are female and the gray is the alpha male."

I walked from the tail to the head and took four big steps and figured it was about 12 feet long. The tail alone was two and a half feet.

Auk told Liq and I to bring the three wolves to the cabin with his dog team and the men will make sure there is no ice in the fishing holes. They will be easy to work on if they don't freeze," he said pointing at the wolves.

I ran to the sled and untied the rope holding Avu to the willows. I lifted the break and turned the team. As we got closer I put the break hook down and Liq started to untie the rope holding the grub box and other hunting gear down. I helped him untie the rawhide rope and we met in the middle. Liq rolled the line up and tied it on the side of the basket sled. We then pulled the tarp with all the hunting gear. The only thing we moved separate was the grub box. We struggled to put the big gray wolf up onto the sled. After we put the big one in, the other two were easier to handle. We tied the three wolves down and walked over to Auk and Savik.

Savik was pulling up a fish as we walked closer. Auk had a few on the ice. He also got a bite and both men pulled up Shii-fish and smiled really big.

They didn't even clean the ice out of Liq and my fishing holes. I grabbed the ax and chopped the ice in my fishing hole. The snow I put on top kept the ice from getting too thick. Soon I cleaned the ice and scooped it out.

As soon as I got done chopping, Liq took the ax and cleaned the ice that formed in his fishing hole. While he was cleaning the last pieces of ice from the water in his hole, I felt a tug on my hook. I pulled up a fish. All four of us pulled Shii-fish out one after another and soon there was a pile in front of Liq and I. We fished with the men until there was enough fish in front of both Liq and I to fill both sleds.

We stopped fishing and put our hooks aside. "We will be back soon with warm coffee in the Thermos," I said to Auk.

Auk pulled up another and before he could put his hook back into the water, his brother, Savik, pulled up a fish. They both smiled and said, "We will be watching for the dog team to come back from the cabin."

Liq and I smiled at each other and walked to the dog team. I went to Avu and untied the line from Avu to a willow. The dogs all wanted to run. They could smell the wolves in the sled and didn't like any wolf, dead or alive.

I lifted the break hook and the dogs pulled us across the snow. We glided around the bend and soon we pulled up alongside of the cabin's front door. I set the break hook and made sure it wouldn't get loose. I tied the line from Avu to the corner of the cabin.

Liq went into the cabin as soon as we stopped. He went to the wood stove and, using a poker, he fired up the coals and added wood that would be easy to catch fire. He put the kettle on the hottest part of the stove and got the coffee pot ready.

After the fire was going good, Liq went back out and helped me drag the three wolves into the cabin. We put the three wolves against the wall on the floor. Liq and I struggled with the big gray wolf and were happy when the wolf was safely inside.

Liq quickly made the Thermos ready by filling it with boiling water. The Thermos had a caribou skin case. The fur was inside and a cloth was sewn over with a tie string at the mouth. We filled the Thermos with hot coffee and both drank a cup before we went back out and got the dog team headed back to the fishing sight.

We stopped the dog team by our own fishing holes. Savik had taken a short break and moved his team by the pile in front of Liq's fishing hole.

I quickly untied the tarp and brought the steaming Thermos full of coffee to Auk. I poured him a cup after I unscrewed it from the top. The four of us filled our cups and Liq opened the moose meat sandwiches he made for everyone. We ate two sandwiches each with the coffee.

The men helped us load the sleds after we all finished our snack. Both our sleds were filled to overflowing. We had to make four or five such trips to move all the fish we caught there.

I watched as Savik helped Liq tie the tarp down onto the sled. He then pushed the sled to get it moving. I then lifted my break hook and Auk pushed the sled with me until the dogs picked up speed. I waived back at Auk and Savik as I turned onto the main river.

We stayed on the trail going to town. The flock of ptarmigan were still across the main river as we came out of the slough. The morning was warming up and there was more and more sunlight as the days wore on.

Liq slowed his dog team until we were side by side. He pointed across the river at the ptarmigan and made a motion like he was shooting a shotgun. He smiled at me as he reached down and held the sled.

I said, "Mayuk will be really jealous when he see us drive by his house." My smile was ear to ear.

Mayuk was a couple years older than Liq and I. He always like to let people know when he get something and will pout for days when Liq and I do anything. That is why it was important Liq and I filled the sleds ourselves. Catching one at a time, we still had time to bring the wolves to camp and bring our fish home before the morning was all gone. The dog team trail went right past his house. It was the first house on the left as you drive into town from the south.

"Oi – Oi," said Liq as we got closer to town. "I might stop by his home and bring one fish to them," he announced with a twinkle in his eyes.

Dogs started barking at us as we got closer. The closer we came, the more dogs barked. Liq turned the dogs to the left and slowed down when he got by Mayuk's place. We both set the break hooks and Liq quickly pulled a couple fish and carried them to Mayuk's front door. He smiled as Keerik (Mayuk's mother) opened the door and gave Liq a hug and said, "Thank you my relative."

Keerik took the fish in the house and Liq and I started the dog teams home. We lived next door to each other and the dogs stopped by the side of the cabins. Our fathers built their caches about 10 feet apart and 10 feet up in the air. The two homes were on each side of the hunters' caches. When we stopped, I was under the door and there was about four feet from the sled to the first step.

I tied Avu down and after I made sure the dog team was not going anywhere, I walked to Liq and together we unloaded his sled. Liq climbed up the ladder and opened the door. He stooped to get in. Once he was inside he could stand up. I then started to throw fish up to him. He would catch a fish and throw it in back. We emptied the sled and went to the other. I climbed up the ladder and Liq threw the fish up. After all the fish were put away, I grabbed one side of the moose hindquarter and Liq picked up the other end. We carried the hindquarter into the front arctic entryway.

When we went inside there was nobody around. The fire was going good in the wood stove, with the kettle and teapot off to the side. Liq and I just smiled and went back to our dogs. Liq turned his team in front of me and scooted down the trail. I lifted the break hook and the team took off after Liq. We raced out of town and waived at Keerik as we sped along on the dog team trail.

Keerik made Liq and I smile really big when she hollered at us as we drove past her house, "I'm letting Mayuk clean them right now."

Yes, my smile bubbled all the way down to my stomach. Liq turned back at me and I could see his teeth as we smiled at each other. The dogs were going about 12 miles an hour and we flew over the trail, both dog teams running smoothly. Liq was about 60 yards in front of me and both sleds were empty. All the dogs got into a rhythm and the miles flew by.

When we got close to the hunting cabin, Liq pointed towards it and turned his team. I followed behind and he had tied the line from his lead dog to the corner of the cabin. I pulled up alongside his team and went a little past, so our dogs wouldn't get tangled. I set the break and tied the line to the willows and the other end on Avu's line.

Liq made another pot of coffee with the Coleman two-burner. We filled the big Thermos and put it back into the caribou skin pouch. We filled a smaller Thermos we kept for short trips. Liq grabbed the Sailor Boy Crackers and the peanut butter and orange marmalade jam. We tied it down in Liq's sled and we closed everything and started towards the fishing spot. The dogs left the hunting cabin with a blast and we soon turned into the slough and could see both men in the same places, but with more fish on the ice.

Liq slowed his team and stopped them over by the willows where he had tied them before. I pulled up behind Liq and quickly tied the line from Avu to a willow.

"Hi. Did you guys go to town yet?" asked Auk as he pulled up another fish. Savik also brought a fish up and smiled.

Liq grabbed the ax and went to his hole and started cleaning the ice and soon he was splashing water. I used the shovel and cleaned the ice and Liq hit the rough edges in the ice. As soon as he cleaned the ice out of his fishing hole Liq walked to me (Quaq) and started to clean the ice in his hole. As soon as it was clean and fixed around the edge, Liq put the ax in the hunting gear and we both started fishing.

It was sometime around noon when the fish slowed down biting. We put our hunting gear on the sleds and as much fish we could put on. We stood on the back of the fully loaded sleds and started going back to camp.

When we reached the cabin we went in and started a fire. We helped each other skin the three wolves. Liq and Savik worked together while

Auk and I quickly skinned another. We got done about the same time and Savik and Auk skinned the big gray.

Liq and I went out and collected wood from the pile behind the cabin and put enough wood inside for the next time we came back. We worked together and cut kindling to make it easier to start the fire in the morning.

When Auk and Savik finished skinning the wolf, we put the plywood on the two windows and put the lock on the cache door. When everything was in order we got behind the sleds and turned the dog team upriver. The sun was shining and our dog team pulled us along the trail. We would make a few more trips to camp to collect all the fish and meat in the cache.

That, my friends, was the best fishing trip we had in a long, long time. Liq and I loaded our shotguns and went after ptarmigan, but that is another story.

The end

(Prequel to the story Three Legged Lemming)

POTLATCH

INUPIAQ ESKIMOS CIRCA 1800S

By Wendell Amisimak Stalker

02-21-2017

This is a work of fiction. Names, characters, places and incidents are either the product of the author's imagination or are used fictitiously, and any resemblance to actual persons, living or dead, business establishments, events or locales is entirely coincidental.

I remember the night she was born. It was winter time when caribou stayed in the valley all year long. The night she was born was clear and cold. The stars could be seen above the dancing Northern Lights. I could hear every step I took on the snow as I walked to my grandfather, Manguq's sod hut. The dogs were restless and barked as I walked past them. I walked up to the dwelling and went into the long entryway. I had to duck a little as I made my way in the dark. As I was about to let people know I had reached, I heard my grandfather bid me come in.

I moved the heavy bear hide that kept the cold out and the heat in. I stepped down and shook the snow off my mukluks and took my big parka off. I looked around and saw all the familiar things I had seen every day. There were three other men in with Manguq.

Sitting by his side was his son, Avlak, and his grandsons sat across from them, Masu and Maliq.

"What he say?" asked Manguq as I sat down by Masu. He put his wooden cup down and looked at me with a smile on his face.

"He said thank you," I replied. "And then he told me to go. I think he was all ready to talk to his animal helping spirits."

We were talking about our village shaman, Winter Cloud. I had delivered a hindquarter of caribou to him.

Manguq had talked with him and they had agreed on caribou meat as a gift for special prayers for the coming child. Manguq had told Winter Cloud to bless the boy that was going to be born into his family.

...

Winter Cloud was in a trance and talked with his spirit helpers. They told him the baby's name and said they would help the child as long as the child walked among men. The child would become known up and down the coast and will live a long life having children and grandchildren, even will get to see great grandchildren.

...

The old woman who hunched over the big extended belly wiped the sweat away from the forehead and moved the pile of furs used as a pillow to make the mother to be a little more comfortable. The sod hut was built as a place for women to have babies. There was a bed and fireplace and fresh water.

She told the two other women to check if the water was warm and be ready to help when the baby come out to meet our world.

The old ladies name was Patchon. She was the village elder and was there when most of the people were born.

Imaq was the mother of Titquaq and they were there to help Patchon deliver Qavlaq's baby. Imaq walked over to the seal oil lamp to fix the moss wick on the edge of the seal oil. As the water was warming up by the edge of the seal oil lamp the two helpers took out a few rabbit skins to soak up some of the blood.

...

Imaq and Qavlaq were sisters and Imaq's husband was the village's best harpoon maker. Qavlaq's husband was out hunting caribou and was expected back anytime, though it was common for hunters to stay a few days. Niqsiq was his name and his hunting partner's name was Qaviq. Niqsiq knew it was almost time for the baby to be born.

...

There were eight hands and four sod huts in the village, and I had helped build every one of them. My name is Uvlaq and my grandfather, Manguq, had us younger men get tundra for the top of each sod hut. I worked alongside my cousin and friend Amaqpuq. We cut slabs off the tundra and put them on top of the frame of each dwelling. Everyone worked together and we enjoyed the last of the summer.

...

Grandfather filled his wooden cup with tundra tea and brought me back from my summer daydream. He cleared his throat and got a little more comfortable on the furs.

"Let me tell you about the child who is to be born into our family. There was an old, old lady named Qoovlu who lived by herself at the edge of the village. This was when I was a boy. She told everyone that there would be a time when the caribou stayed in the valley all year long, in the time when the sun start to stay up in the sky longer than the night, there will be a child born to Manguq's lineage. She told us the name of the child would be revealed at the time of birth. The child would be a wonderful addition to the family and would unite many people. We are going to have a dance for this child when it is born. I have already met with the elders and when the child is born we will all meet at the Community Meeting Place. Our shaman will bring the mother and child at the right time. Make sure everything is ready. Go to every home and tell everyone. It should be soon."

As we started to put our parkas on Manguq stopped Avlak and said, "Wait, we will go see the shaman, Winter Cloud. The young men will go tell everyone the baby is almost here."

I followed Masu and Maliq out and we all went in different directions to spread the news. I had to watch out for all the dogs tied behind the people's homes. The snow made loud noise as I went from home to home letting all the people know of the planned potlatch. More and more, boys went around spreading the good tidings and soon I was back at Manguq's home. That's when I heard Qavlaq's piercing scream, filled with soul splitting shrieks. I looked towards the sod hut and saw our shaman, Winter Cloud, as he stepped out from the entrance. He held two feathers in his left hand and his ceremonial short staff on his right. I heard his bone rattles that were attached to each ankle. He looked up towards the moon and chanted, shaking the feathers and his staff. He stopped and made a jester as if he was asking the unseen spirits why. Then Manguq came out followed by Avlak. Manguq went to Winter Cloud and also put his arms up. All three men looked pretty upset. Qavluq's screaming stopped suddenly and Winter Cloud fell on his backside onto the snow.

Then it dawned on me. The baby was born. I ran towards the three men as the two younger women came out of the sod hut and saw them quickly walk away from the three men. The two disappeared around the sod hut and I looked at Winter Cloud, who was still sitting on the snow. When I got close enough to see his face, I could see unbelief written all over it. He kept saying over and over, "He's a she, he's a she."

"What?" hollered Manguq. "What do you mean by he's a she?"

"The baby," muttered Winter Cloud. "The spirits told me her name will be Three Legged Lemming!"

"We are still having the potlatch for my granddaughter!" Manguq would not be more proud when he repeated the announcement. "Who are we to go against our ancestors!"

Winter Cloud sat on the snow for a little while until the words of Manguq were understood. He jumped up and started a wild dance and with a smile on his face, he proclaimed the babies name, Three Legged Lemming, three times in each direction. He then looked towards the people who were starting to gather. "The spirits have seen fit to bestow upon us this day, the best year for all of us here by expecting this special, special child. The potlatch will be tonight! Hurry and gather all the people in the village and meet at the Community Meeting Place!"

As I started back to Manguq's home, I heard dogs at the edge of the village barking and saw two dog teams coming through the sod homes. They were Niqsiq and Qavig with both sleds piled high with caribou. The dogs struggled to pull the heavy loads as they came up the last little snowbank and stopped. I had helped raise the dogs and Niqsiq's lead dog, Avu, and I had slept together many times when he was growing up. Avu jumped up and tried to kiss my face. I turned to the side and he licked my cheek. I wiped it off and told him, "Get down."

All the dogs in the village were barking and we had to talk loud. Niqsiq put his hook down to keep the dog team from getting away. He put his hood back and tied his mittens behind his back. The mittens were attached to each other by a line. He walked to me and gave me a big hug. His smiling teeth glowed in the arctic dusk.

"Hi, Uvlaq. How you doing my little Bug Hopping?" He used the nickname he gave me when we looked down from a hill one spring and we saw something hopping down on the ice below us.

I had pointed at the little black dot far down below and said, "Look, a little bug hopping." When we got down there we saw it was a muskrat jumping around on the ice.

"What did you snag today, Niqsiq?" I asked as we were both surrounded by the people. The dogs were taken care of first and the loaded sleds were emptied and the empty sleds put up on a rack. The caribou were put in the underground cellars after the intestines were removed. With a lot of hands, it took a few minutes to put all the hunting gear away. As we were doing everything, I had told Niqsiq of his new baby. He smiled while I told him what I had heard. He laughed when I told him our shaman, Winter Cloud, had landed on his backside and how he had jumped up and said the new baby's name three times in each direction. The shaman told us the baby's name would be Three Legged Lemming.

"I am very proud of my new baby," said Niqsiq. "Just look at all the fresh caribou meat Qaviq and I brought back. She is already a provider!" He walked in front of us and we all stopped outside of the birthing sod hut. He ducked into the entrance and we all stood around under the moon and stars.

We walked to our homes and started getting ready for the potlatch. I took off my warm parka and put it aside. Then I went to my sleeping place and dug out my ceremonial coat and got it ready to put on. As soon as everything to eat was ready, Manguq and I started bringing foods of every kind out of the cellar and a sled was used to bring it all to the Community Meeting Place. After we unloaded the sled, I ran back home and put my fancy coat on. It was made by Patchon and was bleached pure white. She had attached many seashells in a beautiful pattern. There were fringes hanging all around it and I put on the ivory necklace I had won playing Eskimo games. It was walrus ivory with a miniature stone lamp on the bottom. I put my dancing gloves in my front pocket and changed my mukluks. I then put the stone cover on the seal oil lamp and took my drum and beater.

Their joy at coming together for a baby was something nobody in the village would want to miss. I walked to the Community Meeting Place with two brothers who had both grandparents in their sled. The elders greeted me and Somiq said he brought his drum also. His wife, Qonaq, giggled in front of him and we saw many people all headed for the Community Meeting Place. People were scurrying around getting in each others way until Winter Cloud came to the sod hut with Niqsiq pushing a sled with Qavlaq all bundled up holding the sides of the sled. The baby was inside the back of Qavlaq's parka, staying warm against her mother's back.

The people moved to the sides and made room for the shaman, Winter Cloud, who pulled out his Snowy Owl caller and made loud screeches by blowing on one end of his tube-like object. The noise was like a Snowy Owl as he looked here and there. He led Niqsiq and Qavlaq into the big meeting place. There were people already inside who made room. Winter Cloud walked to the center and stopped. He then called out to the people and invited Niqsiq and Qavlaq to sit down by him. He put his Snowy Owl caller away and made himself comfortable, his bone rattles finally quiet.

Qavlaq untied the strap that held the baby inside her parka. She then pulled her right arm in, out of the sleeve, and reached back for the baby. When she had a good grip on the infant, she pushed the parka off and that was the first time everyone saw the baby.

Oh...she was a beauty. Her head was dark with hair. Everything about her was perfect. Tiny little fingers and toes, pug nose and clear, dark brown eyes. When she cried the crowd let out some oohs and aahs.

Three other women brought their babies over and sat close by. The smiles of two older babies got everyone talking and laughing.

"Your baby have more hair than all these babies put together," exclaimed Putiq, who was holding one of the other babies.

"Look, Sila, you're not going to be alone," said Evalou, as she held her little girl closer to Three Legged Lemming.

The other mothers all laughed and started feeding their babies, as more people came into the Community Meeting Place. The big room was very warm after being outside. Most of the people sat by the walls where there was a ledge to sit on. Many had their finest clothing on and the best ivory jewelry was on display. Even the poorest people had nice things to show because when a hunter got more than his family needed, they gave it to the elders and widows.

Winter Cloud stood up as soon as he got a nod from me. I was by the entrance and let him know when all the people had arrived.

"Qii..." Winter Cloud said in a loud voice. "Everyone is here. Let us start by having Qavlaq stand up and show everyone our new baby!"

Qavlaq stood up and, using one hand, she moved her long hair to one side and lifted Three Legged Lemming up in the air for everyone to see. She looked very tired and didn't stay standing long, but everyone had a good look at the newborn baby. She sat down with a big smile when she heard the eldest man call the baby "Little Mom ma."

Winter Cloud said, "Let us all make this child welcome. This special one is very welcome because Qoovlu had told us, when the caribou stayed in the valley all year long a baby would be born into Manguq's family."

The people were in awe even some had heard the news before and there were a few people who had been there and remembered Qoovlu.

"Let us enjoy the feast and after we will have dancing and games!" said our shaman as he gave the go ahead to us young men and women to start serving.

Amaqpuq and I worked together and started handing out food from a huge wooden platter. We started by bringing the food to Winter Cloud and Manguq, then we went in a circle until it was empty. We walked back and filled it three more times and other young people partnered up and did the same.

There was fish of all kinds, along with different meats from both land and sea. The most was caribou that every hunter brought in. We gave moose, bear, and mountain sheep. A few ducks and eggs were given to our elders, along with salmon eggs that were dried after most of the flesh was taken off. There was rabbit and ptarmigan and Snowy Owl. We brought in a seal poke full of oil and different kinds of sea food in it. In the poke, there was white Beluga whale and Bowhead whale with seal meat and walrus, dried fish, cooked black and white muktuk, willow greens and roots. We also gave salmon berries, blueberries, blackberries, and cranberries. We brought in another poke filled with Eider ducks which had been cooked, then put in seal oil pokes. The pokes were made from the whole skin of a seal. The women would start from the mouth of a seal and would separate the flesh without making any holes. The skin was then turned inside out and the excess flesh cleaned off. After it was cleaned, they would make a wooden plug, put the meat in and filled it full of seal oil. The plug was tied with rawhide string, and put in underground cellars to freeze until ready to be eaten.

Amaqpuq and I sat down to eat after most of the food was given out. We had put some aside for the young adults who did the serving. Everyone there had more than they could eat and laughter could be heard. The people were all happy. From the oldest to the youngest, we ate and ate, until we could eat no more.

As I drank my second bowl of tundra tea, I gave a huge burp and leaned back. My stomach was full and I knew everyone there was just as full as I was, yet there was still more food. I looked around and noticed our shaman, Winter Cloud, going behind a curtain.

Niqsiq went to the seal oil lamps and, putting a cover on each one, made the Community Meeting Place darker. We all kind-of quit talking and everyone sat down. Niqsiq left one lamp on, then went back to his seat. The darkest place was by the curtain where Winter Cloud had casually disappeared behind.

People whispered, then everyone heard a noise like a wind blowing. The curtain then started moving. First, it was just a little on the left corner.

The curtain was made of caribou skins sewn together, after all the hair was taken off. It covered one side of the huge Community Meeting Place, and I knew it was about wide enough for me to touch the wall and the curtain. I also knew there was no exit behind it.

The curtain started moving more and more and the sound of the wind got louder. People started moving away from the curtain and everyone who didn't see Winter Cloud go back there was really confused.

Then all of a sudden the curtain quit moving and the sound of the wind stopped. It got very quiet in the semidarkness. We then heard Winter Cloud's ankle rattles. It sounded like he was walking closer. The rattles were very easy to hear, being made of caribou bones, from the feet, just behind the hooves.

I expected to see Winter Cloud step out from behind the curtain. I then heard his Snowy Owl caller. Then I heard an Eskimo drum. The sound of the drum came from behind me and when I looked back, there was only my drum and the wall. It was not my drum making noise. I looked around and everyone was looking to see who was beating the drum. We all felt like someone was beating the drum right behind us.

The sudden stopping of the drum let the hair on my neck stand up. It was then I heard Winter Cloud's ankle rattles. They sounded like he was walking closer and closer. Soon the curtain moved aside and I thought I would see him come out, but there was nobody there. The curtain dropped back and I could hear the rattles. It scared me when nobody was there. They sounded like Winter Cloud had walked across the room. People really started getting scared, they started to move restlessly until Winter Cloud called from behind the curtain. His voice made me jump because I was looking across the room like everybody there.

"See the smile on the baby, Three Legged Lemming," said Winter Cloud. He then moved the curtain aside and pointed to Three Legged Lemming, who indeed was smiling. Her eyes twinkled and her smile seemed to light the whole place up.

I also saw Qavlaq's eyes as they changed from fear to joy. Fear because everyone thought a ghost had visited, then joy and love as she saw her daughter, Three Legged Lemming, with a huge smile on her pretty little baby face.

Winter Cloud let out a huge burp and started laughing. At first, he was the only one laughing, then the baby, Three Legged Lemming, gave a very cute little giggle. There were some ahs and oohs, then more and more people joined in the laughter.

Winter Cloud then walked to Manguq and picked up his drum and said, "Let us sing and dance now."

I grabbed my drum and walked over to them. Somiq and Qonaq came over and Somiq sat down on the floor. Qonaq went and stood behind him. He was our drumming leader and soon the other drummers sat by him, the ones with wives sat alongside of Somiq and the women stood behind them.

Manguq sat on the floor on the right side of Somiq to show everyone the gathering was in honor of his family. Niqsiq sat at Manguq's right while Qavlaq stayed sitting where she would be able to see all the drummers and singers. Winter Cloud sat to the left of Somiq where the Head Shaman is always sitting. Other drummers sat on both sides, with the elders in the middle and the youngest drummers on the outside.

We talked and laughed as we moved to our places and Amaqpuq sat by me. We made our drums ourselves, starting by hunting to get the skin for our drums. We had hunted for walrus and were able to make the wooden frame and beater only after we caught a walrus. I was very proud of my drum, as Amaqpuq was, I'm sure. Manguq had instructed me from beginning to the finishing touches. I had inlaid the handle with some of the ivory from the same walrus. He showed me how to bend the wood to make a loop and put the walrus jawbone handle on. He held the drums while I tied the walrus stomach membrane onto the wooden hoop. He also taught me how to make the long, thin beater. He put water on the skin so it wouldn't make a hole when it is hit with the beater.

Soon everyone was ready. The people had taken their places, with men sitting on the floor holding their drums. Some were putting water on the drums and would hit it with the beater to make sure it had enough. The people sat on the outside, making room for the dancers. Everyone had a look of excitement, and laughter burst out often.

Winter Cloud stood up and stomped his feet a couple times. We heard his bone rattles and got quiet. Even the children got quiet. He smiled as he looked around. He lifted his drum and hit it three times, then said, "We come together to welcome this beautiful child, Three Legged Lemming. This is the one who Qoovlu told us about a long time ago. Qoovlu let everyone know that someday there will be caribou here all year long. We see that today. The two hunters, Niqsiq and Qaviq, both loaded their sleds today. Now you all know the sun is staying up longer than the night. That is when Qoovlu said there will be a baby born into Manguq's family. The baby would be known up and down the coast and would unite many people. Now let us come together as one and let this beautiful baby, who was given to us from Attiniq who is the creator of every living thing. See how happy we are to be alive today. Thank you Somiq, I give this time back to you." He then sat down and our drumming leader started a slow beat on his drum. We picked up the beaters and all the drummers followed his lead. The drummers slowly used the one-two beat. After the song was done, Somiq looked at Manguq and started the song that was in Manguq's family for generations. Manguq put down his drum and beater. Then reached in his pocket and put on his dancing gloves. He then walked in front of the drummers and faced them. We sang the song quietly and

Manguq made slight motions with his hands and body. The timing of the song did not change. When we got to the end of the song, we started the song over, but the second time we hit our drums louder and sang louder. Manguq turned around and, keeping time with his right foot, he made the words of the song come alive, with motions of his hands and body. Telling a story of a Polar bear hunt that one of our ancestors had taught.

Each motion coincided with the words we sang. Though our ancestor was long dead we all knew exactly how he had killed the Polar bear. It was one way the Inupiaq tell stories that were remembered and retaught over long periods of time. Though we had no written language, we could still know how to survive in our harsh Arctic world.

The words and Manguq's motions brought to life the image of one looking down into a hole in the ice while holding a fishing spear, concentrating on trying to spear fish until his dogs started barking. He then ran to his sled and grabbed his bear-spear, which was about the length of three grown men. There was a donut shaped piece of wood, about a foot and a half from the tip. He then got on one knee and waited for the Polar bear to come to him. Whenever the big bear tried to turn, he would holler and move the spear. When the bear got closer, it tried to push the spear aside, but the hunter kept the point of the spear right in front of the bear's heart. The bear grabbed the do-nut and gave it a huge bear hug and pulled the sharp spear right into it's own heart. Then the hunter danced around with great joy and pride.

After we finished the song, Manguq told his family to come and do the dance with him. Masu, Malik and I went down to stand by Manguq's side. Avlak went on the other side of him and the women came and stood about five feet in front of the men. Imaq and Qavlaq were sisters and Imaq came out, but Qavlaq was still weak from giving birth, but would do the motions while sitting with baby, Three Legged Lemming. Patchon was Manguq's sister so she came to stand in front of him. Titquaq also came out and stood by her mother Imaq.

We did the motions in the first singing halfheartedly. Then when the second singing started, we all acted out the family dance. Each of us moving our hands and bodies in pantomime, acting out the hunting of the fish and hearing the dogs barking, and running to the sled to grab the bear spear. Going down on one knee and shouting to attract the bear, the joy after the big bear was dead. Everyone danced the motions as if we were attached to the movements of Grandpa Manguq. The only noticeable difference was how us men kept time with the drumming. The men would stomp their right foot in time with the drumming while the women would bend at the knees. Qavlak had stayed down with Three Legged Lemming and did the hand and body motions with us, and the baby had fallen back asleep before I sat down to my drum.

As soon as everyone was seated, Somiq looked at Winter Cloud and pointed his beater at him. That way everyone would know who is to dance next. When Winter Cloud saw Somiq pointing the stick at him, he looked here and there as if to see if Somiq was pointing at someone else sitting by him. He then smiled and slowly stood up. He put his drum down and bent over the drum where nobody could see, and quickly put elaborate dancing gloves on and put on a dark robe that covered his whole body. When he lifted his head we could see the beak of a Raven. Somiq had already started to sing the song they had practiced in Winter Cloud's sod hut. Nobody had heard the song before, and only the one-two beat kept me quietly playing along with the other drummers. As Somiq sang a song of a raven flying up to a hunter who was working on a dog harness, Winter Cloud kept time with the drumming one-two beat. We all saw a huge raven hop out seeming to peck here and another peck there. When the second singing of the song began, the huge raven flew to the hunter and told him he knew where some caribou were. The hunter kept working on the dog harness and that made the raven fly away and he went to another hunter far away and told the hunter he knew where there were caribou.

The hunter said, "I will give you the eyes if you show me where to hunt caribou." The raven danced around with joy and got the hunter pointed in the right direction.

The dog team soon got to where the caribou were and after the hunter got some caribou, he left the eyes for the raven. And the raven ate and ate. The hunter put meat away and filled his dog sled full of choice meats. He thanked the raven and told him he would be back for the rest of the caribou meat.

The raven could barely fly, he was so full. He flew over the first hunter who had finally fixed the harness and was still looking for caribou. The raven cawed a couple times and landed close by. The hunter drove right by and didn't know he was going the wrong way.

"I know where the caribou are," said the raven over and over, but the hunter disappeared down the coast.

The raven turned back into Winter Cloud when the song was over. He just slipped the robe off and took the raven hood with beak off at the same time. He smiled and we heard each step of his bone rattles as he walked back to his drum by Somiq. Each movement of our shaman, Winter Cloud, was as a real bird had been in front of us and when he sat down, it got quiet for a little while, until Somiq pointed his beater at Avlak. And we watched Manguq's son do a fine seal hunt out in open water using a kayak.

"Ah – ya – ya ah – ya," sang the people and the drums booming sound vibrated into the arctic night. Our spirits were uplifted and all fear was gone. As different dancers went out to perform, the vastness of our world was compressed into one big sod hut. We were one with each other and with nature.

The dances and songs brought life, knowledge, and wisdom from ancestors long dead. We watched the dancers and sang the songs. We beat the drums and felt the same as the old ones have felt. We showed the whole world, this is our heritage, this is who I am, and this land is as much a part of me as I am a part of this community. We live in harmony with nature, being one with the land, sea and weather. We move in seasonal hunts, going where the animals were. Our world was celebrated through song and dance after eating the best foods all taken by hunting and food gathering.

Somiq told the young men to do the walrus dance and after that it would be common dance.

I put my drum down and put my dancing mittens on. Amaqpuq, Masu, Maliq, and Putiq, 'our young friend who came to our village the year before,' all walked out to the dance floor. The five of us had worked with Manguq and made walrus masks. We stood in line and started the motions when Somiq started the song. At the end, we got everyone there all clapping when Putiq ran a few steps in front and did the motions different. That was the first time we saw someone from a far-off land move like a walrus moving on land.

We sat down and Somiq started the common dances where everyone who wanted could go out and dance. Young and old went out and danced, showing joyous expressions of life. We did a few songs that everyone knew and when they were done, we hugged with joy and laughter.

Somiq started the last dance by calling all the older hunters. Salmon Head walked out, followed by three hands of hunters. All wore the traditional labret at the ends of the mouth. A hole was made and an ivory plug was put in. The older one got, the bigger the labret, because the hole on the side of the chin stretched.

Somiq started a chant without any words, and all the hunters started their own dances. Each dancer told his own story through acting out the important things that happened in their life. We beat the drums in the one-two beat and chanted.

Manguq danced and showed the family story. His labret had grown four times the original size. He moved gracefully and acted out the killing of a giant Polar bear. His son, Avlak, danced by his side. He, too, was proud of the labret, though his was smaller. Avlak did the hunt for walrus and showed the people the ivory he had carved from one of the tusks of the walrus. He was dancing his own motions full of pride and vitality of youth.

Salmon Head danced and told the tale of days gone by. His was the dance of remembrance. He brought to life different elders of the community who had passed on to the great beyond. He acted out a handful of relatives of Manguq's paternal lineage. How great had been the acts of the last few generations as they paved the way to our present community. He was one of a handful who told stories, and he had a lot of native folklore to share.

As the last beats of the drums echoed into the night, we put away our drums and Amaqpuq helped as we put our hides to the side and made the seats more comfortable. Soon the middle of the room was empty. We then started chanting people of the south against the people of the north. We all got quiet when we heard our shaman's rattles as he stomped his feet to get attention. Winter Cloud blew on his owl whistle and then he lifted up his drum. He started a beat that everyone there knew. It was the gift-giving beat.

Some old lady let out one quick burst of laughter, then got quiet when her brother touched her arm. They were the first to give a gift to the baby, Three Legged Lemming. The old lady gave the baby a little sleeping bag made from muskrat skins, with rabbit fur lining. She also gave a bunch of grass for baby's bottom. Her brother gave her a little bag made from seal skin and inside he pulled out an ivory pendant in the likeness of a wolf. The brother then patiently walked his sister back to their seats. As soon as they sat down, another old lady said "Qi" and someone escorted her as they brought gifts. All the while, the shaman was gently beating his drum.

Soon the pile of gifts was getting pretty high. There was another pile of grass that every woman gave as part of the ritual of gift-giving. There was also a pile in front of Winter Cloud. Never had anyone seen so many gifts for a baby girl. It took a while for all the people to put their gifts on the floor.

When the last young people gave gifts, Winter Cloud made the sound of his beating drum fade until it was quiet. He then lifted his voice and told the people, "the spirits told me to give all the gifts to the baby. Here, you young people help me move these gifts over."

When he got close to the baby, he said to Qavlaq, "I'm sorry, I don't have no grass, but here is my gift." He held out a stone scent burner, along with several kinds of incense to burn. He also gave a little fire making kit.

He lifted his hands up in the air and said, "Listen, the spirits told me Three Legged Lemming will need all these gifts to unite all the people. We all must help this baby and watch as the life of this baby be a great help to everyone. The spirits have spoken. Let the games begin."

We separated the young and let the children have part of the floor. Avlak gathered them around and let the ones from the south go to his right and the ones from the north, to his left. There were a few more from up north, but everyone was happy. There were about the same amount of both sexes.

Avlak called the two youngest girls and Pooq and Little Murr walked in front. They were about five seasons old. Avlak had the two girls sit on the floor and face each other. He then had Pooq put her right leg over Murr's left leg, and had Murr put her right over Pooq's left. Avlak then had them cross their right arms in front and hold the right knee of the opponent. He made sure everything was centered then told the girls to pull.

At first, the two girls sat there pulling with all their might. Then slowly, Little Murr started to pull Pooq. Once Murr started to feel Pooq give, she never let up. Little Murr was declared the winner. The people from the north shouted and congratulated Little Murr. When the girls stood up, Pooq looked like she was going to cry until Little Murr reached out and gave her a big hug. Pooq smiled as she walked back to her mother.

Little Murr sat back down and Iqah walked up to her and, rolling her parka sleeve up, she showed her muscles. She sat down and Avlak got them ready. When he gave the go ahead, the girls both made a huge effort, but Little Murr won again. Iqah said, "Adii," and smiled at Little Murr before she walked back to her family. The people from up north all clapped their hands and shouted happy encouraging words.

Apou was asleep when her mother gently woke her up. She had fallen asleep during the gift giving. Her mother's name was Aim-mak, and she asked Apou if she wanted to play Eskimo games. The little girl looked around wiping her sleepy eyes. "What?" she asked. "Look, that girl is winning the arm pull," said Aim-mak. "Go see if you could pull her arm off."

Apou slowly walked toward Little Murr, rubbing the sleep from her eyes. Avlak got them ready and gave them the go ahead. The girls didn't move for a while, then started leaning to one side. Avlak stopped them, and got them ready a second time. When they started pulling again, the people all started hollering.

"Go, go, go," they hollered and screamed as the two girls pulled. Slowly, Little Murr pulled Apou until Avlak said, "The winner is Little Murr."

"Mark," said Avlak, when no more girls came out from the south.

Then it was the girls who were a little older. The young boys had just started and two young guys walked out to face each other. The girls and boys both put on a good show and everyone was happy.

As the evening wore on, we cheered our favorite on. Sometimes someone from the north would cheer for a close friend or relative, even if they came from the south. Our voices rang out and the Northern Lights came out overhead. Throughout the evening, we all got a chance to compete.

Three Legged Lemming slept snuggled up to Qavlaq. Little Murr walked over to see the baby and with a look that was full of adoration, she took the necklace from her neck and said, "Three Legged Lemming might need this to bring the people together someday!" She lay the little dog carved out of ivory on the baby.

Qavlaq tried to give it back, saying, "You won that playing games!"

But Little Murr said, "It will be for all the people to see. Three Legged Lemming got the first trophy on her first day on earth!" Little Murr then gave Qavlaq a hug and walked to her family.

I walked with two brothers, Nipit and Qulaq, as they pushed the sled. Somiq and Qonaq looked tired, but happy, as they rode in the sled. I carried my drum and beater and turned to Manguq's sod hut.

"Good night," said Somiq and I waived to them and said good night to them all.

I went in and changed my parka. I didn't want my nice ceremonial coat to get dirty and I ran back to the Community Meeting Place to help Manguq and the family put things away. There was a lot of people to help Niqsiq and Qavlaq bring baby home.

We put the last seal oil lamp out and made our way home. The Northern Lights were out, all the dogs were lying down, sleeping. The snow crunched under our mukluks as we pushed the sled. The runners made a ringing sound on the snow.

I yawned as we got the last of the leftover food put away. Manguq had already gone to bed. Maliq and Masu helped me put the last seal poke up the ten foot ladder. The poke was made from a bearded seal that was eight hundred pounds. Even we had eaten a lot from it, the poke was still heavy. The seal oil had warmed up while we ate and danced. We then played games and finally brought the seal poke out using the sled. We finally wrestled the big seal poke over by the others up in the cache. I closed the door and put the latch on.

As I climbed down the ladder, I smiled real big and thought, I will remember today as long as I live because of a baby called Three Legged Lemming.

The end

TOUCHED AT FORTY MILES ABOVE THE ARCTIC CIRCLE

By Wendell Amisimak Stalker

January 9, 2019

This is a work of fiction. Names, characters, places and incidents are either the product of the author's imagination or are used fictitiously, and any resemblance to actual persons, living or dead, business establishments, events or locales is entirely coincidental.

It was a clear spring day. The flowers were blooming and there was a gentle wind coming from the south. The temp was in the mid 70's and the sun would stay up for 24 hours every day. It may cool off to about 50 degrees above zero in the early morning hours, but always climbed back up to the mid 70's around lunch time.

I watched the young Eskimo girl take her windbreaker coat off and hold it in front of her. She slowly approached a Monarch butterfly that had landed a few feet in front of her. When she was right over the yellow butterfly she simply dropped her coat on top and she had a live Monarch under it.

A bee buzzed me and I watched it fly to a big field of yellow buttercups. I slapped my cheek when I felt a mosquito bite. There was a spot of blood on my hand, so I knew I got that one. I wiped it on my sleeve as I watched the young girl slowly roll the coat along the edge.

She moved real quickly, then I saw her hold up the Monarch butterfly. It looked bigger than her hand. She then walked to me and showed me the beautiful big black and yellow butterfly. She had smashed the head and killed it by accident. She told me she was going to put it in her Grandma's Bible.

She sat by me and asked if I had gone to church that Sunday. I replied, "No, I didn't go."

She laughed and said, "Some old lady fell asleep up on the second pew. The piano player opened the Hymn book in front of her and said, "Page 50 in your hymn book. 5-Oh." The old lady sleeping up in the second pew stood up suddenly and raising her hand up in the air she hollered at the top of her lungs, "Bingo!"

The first one to start laughing was the visiting Pastor. Then our Pastor joined him laughing out loud. Soon everyone in the church was laughing. I laughed so hard until I touched someone laying in the middle of the aisle. I didn't know when I got on the floor, but I just kept being tickled by someone I couldn't see. I don't remember when the service ended, but I remember kind of floating home laughing all the way. There was a really mean Husky dog tied close by the drying racks. It would bark at me and bare it's teeth. I laughed at it and when I got closer, it started growling. I laughed and said in a commanding voice, "Peace. Be still." The big dog immediately sat down and stuck his tongue out the side of his mouth. I laughed and continued my walk home from the canvas covered church here in the middle of our hunting grounds.

Now, every time something goes wrong, I laugh the laugh I learned in church on Sunday and whatever is wrong will get fixed. I think you should go to church on Sunday morning. It is the one with the 55-gallon drum in front of it. We don't have a bell so the Pastor will bang on the drum with a piece of two by four. Please come and learn how the Lord works. Even forty miles above the Arctic Circle He could give you Holy laughter and you can walk around laughing at anything that goes wrong and the Holy Spirit will make it right.

She looked into my eyes and I saw love. That was the only way I could explain it. She laughed as she looked into my eyes and I got this beautiful urge to laugh with her. I laughed and laughed. I laughed as she walked away holding the beautiful Monarch butterfly. I laughed as she went into a canvas tent with a 55-gallon drum in front of it. I laughed and gently removed a mosquito from my cheek that was poking me. I laughed even harder when I saw the mosquito fly away.

I laughed the week away and on Sunday morning, I was the first one in the canvas tent when the Pastor banged on the 55-gallon drum for first bell. By the time he started hitting the drum for second bell, everyone in the canvas covered church was laughing and laughing.

Please...oh, please come to the canvas covered church and learn how the Lord is moving. Please come and learn to laugh the Holy laughter. It's the one with the empty 55-gallon drum in front. It's 40 miles above the Arctic Circle, you can't miss it.

Ha-ha ha ha ha ha....

Another funny thing. I never did see that young girl again, but when I looked into an old and well-used Bible, I saw a Monarch butterfly. It looks as colorful and alive as the day she first brought it to me. Let me see, about 60 years ago, if I remember right.

Ha-ha ha-ha ha-ha ha....

The end.

CPSIA information can be obtained
at www.ICGtesting.com
Printed in the USA
BVHW072236050123
655708BV00003B/8

9 781646 205745